THE
WOLVES

OF GREYCOAT HALL

First American Edition 2023
Kane Miller, A Division of EDC Publishing.

Text and illustrations © 2020 Lucinda Gifford
Published by arrangement with Walker Books Limited, London.

For information contact:
Kane Miller, A Division of EDC Publishing
5402 S. 122nd E. Ave, Tulsa, OK 74146
www.kanemiller.com

Library of Congress Control Number: 2022950463

Printed and bound in the United States of America
1 2 3 4 5 6 7 8 9 10
ISBN: 978-1-68464-719-4

THE
WOLVES
OF GREYCOAT HALL

LUCINDA GIFFORD

Kane Miller
A DIVISION OF EDC PUBLISHING

For my parents, James and Pat.

CONTENTS

The McLupus Family Tree

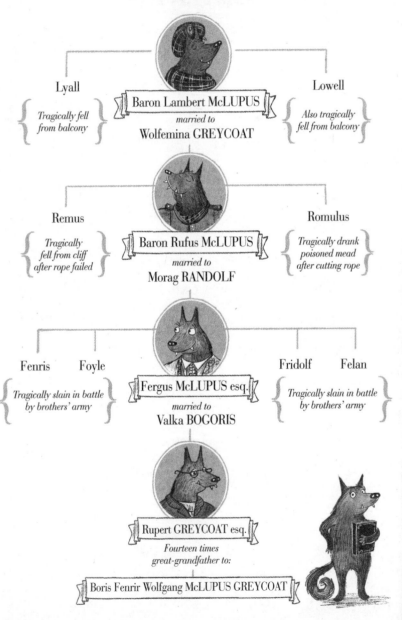

Baron Lambert McLUPUS
married to
Wolfemina GREYCOAT

Lyall
{ *Tragically fell from balcony* }

Lowell
{ *Also tragically fell from balcony* }

Baron Rufus McLUPUS
married to
Morag RANDOLF

Remus
{ *Tragically fell from cliff after rope failed* }

Romulus
{ *Tragically drank poisoned mead after cutting rope* }

Fergus McLUPUS esq.
married to
Valka BOGORIS

Fenris Foyle
{ *Tragically slain in battle by brothers' army* }

Fridolf Felan
{ *Tragically slain in battle by brothers' army* }

Rupert GREYCOAT esq.
Fourteen times great-grandfather to:

Boris Fenrir Wolfgang McLUPUS GREYCOAT

This is Boris. He is a friendly young wolf who likes meeting people and trying new foods.

This is Boris's father, Randall Greycoat, who is a polymath. A polymath is someone who is an expert in lots of things. Here is Randall becoming an expert in speaking French and playing table tennis.

Boris's mother is called Leonora Greycoat. Right now, she is looking in the mirror and practicing her warm, reassuring smiles. Wolves need to look reassuring if they are to flourish in society.

Like most wolves, the Greycoats live in the forest. Not in a den or a cave, but in Greycoat Hall, a fancy mansion with twenty-three turrets. Greycoat Hall is in the little-known Principality of Morovia, which is a popular place for respectable wolves to live.

Here is a wolf cake, baked by the famous wolf chefs of Morovia. To make Morovian wolf cake, you will need flour, salt, pig fat, and (worst of all) coconut. Once baked, the cake is iced and decorated with silver sparkles. Wolf cake looks delicious, but sadly it is not.

One of the things that Boris and his parents like most is going on vacation. Traveling abroad is a wonderful opportunity for respectable wolves to learn about other cultures, and to enjoy properly delicious cakes.

CHAPTER 1

A Summer Vacation

In the parlor of Greycoat Hall, afternoon tea was being served. Young wolf Boris Greycoat sat opposite a scrumptious-looking mound of scones, muffins and tea cakes. Unfortunately the cakes were rock hard and tasted of old coconut.

Ugh! thought Boris, as he gnawed on a heavy scone.

As if the scone wasn't bad enough, his parents were "having a discussion" about where to go for summer vacation. ("Having a discussion" is grown-up wolf talk for arguing–but politely.)

"Darling!" said Leonora, Boris's mother. "Not France again! Remember Paris!"

"My French has improved since then, my love," said Randall. "Next time I go to a French restaurant, I will take care to ask **WHAT** is for dinner, not **WHO** is for dinner."

"It was an easy mistake to make, Dad," said Boris. Boris wanted to be kind, as he knew his father considered himself good at languages.

But Boris was worried. Last year, after the Greycoats vacationed in France, the mayor of Paris had put out a notice: "Beware wolves in tailored clothing!"

This time, Boris wanted to go to a country where wolves were welcome. But where?

Then he saw it! Next to a half-chewed muffin lay a copy of *The Lupine Times*.

"Mum! Dad!" said Boris. "Look at the news!"

He picked up the paper and read aloud:

WOLVES TO BE REINTRODUCED TO SCOTLAND

Since 1680, there have been no wolves in Scotland. But now The Scottish Royal Conservation Society wishes to welcome us back. Wolves will be reintroduced, starting with the Highlands and islands. Perhaps, one day soon, we wolves can go about our daily lives in Scottish cities without shrieks of terror from the local population.

His parents were staring at one another.

"My dears," said Leonora, "what wonderful news!"

Boris knew his family had Scottish connections. On the walls of Greycoat Hall hung lots of Scottish-looking paintings. There were romantic, outdoorsy Scottish paintings, with brave-looking wolves standing in front of mountains.

And murky, indoorsy Scottish paintings, with serious-looking wolves sipping whisky by the fire.

"We're sort of Scottish, aren't we?" Boris asked his parents.

Leonora and Randall were smiling at him, their eyes bright.

"Why," said Randall, "not just sort of! We have distinguished Scottish heritage. Now! Enough chitchat. I must read more!"

While Randall and Leonora read the rest of the article, Boris looked through *The Lupine Times* weekend magazine. He was happy to find an article on Scottish food, featuring photographs of fruitcake, shortbread, berry jam and light, crumbly scones.

"Why don't we go to Scotland this summer?" he asked.

At this, Randall gave a low growl and placed his front paws on his lap.

When Randall put his paws on his lap, it meant he was about to make a Dramatic Statement. Leonora and Boris watched nervously. In the Greycoat family, Randall's Dramatic Statements often led to Sticky Situations.

"Of course we should go!" declared Randall. He leaped from his chair and stood by the mantelpiece, his paw on his chest. "If wolves are to be reintroduced, we must seek an introduction! We, the Greycoats, shall show the Scottish people how wonderful wolves can be. I propose that we travel to Scotland, our ancestral homeland, on the next available train!"

On the next train! Boris dropped his scone in surprise. It bounced on the floor and crashed into an urn, causing several deep cracks to appear.

But Leonora nodded calmly. "Well, why not?" she said. "There are no romantic glens here in Morovia and the cakes are shocking. And I could do with a nice tartan suit. How clever you are with your ideas, my dear.

"Now I must make some calls," she said, making her way toward the Great Hall. "I will get in touch with the embassy without delay."

CHAPTER 2

The Trans-Bohemia Express

Of course, Boris and his parents didn't take the train to Scotland that very afternoon. Wolves need to pack and put their affairs in order before traveling, especially to somewhere new. But Leonora was excellent at organizing and so, just before teatime the following Saturday, the Greycoats were at Morovia Central Station with their suitcases, waiting to board the Trans-Bohemia Express.

Boris had packed his day bag with just a few traveling essentials: a sketchbook, a pencil set, his tartan dressing gown, a tin of salted caramels and a large, leather-bound book – *The History of the*

Scottish Greycoats by Baron McLupus the Fifteenth. Randall had found the book in the Greycoat Hall library. It was all about the Greycoats' Scottish ancestors, he'd told Boris, and had lots of battles,  betrayals and Dangerous Misunderstandings.

The wolves planned to spend all summer in Scotland. "This train travels through Europe, up to Rotterdam, on the Dutch coast," Leonora explained as their baggage was being collected. "It's a long trip, so we'll sleep overnight in our own special cabin. Then we'll get the overnight ferry to England, where we'll sleep in another cabin. The morning after that, we'll take a train to Scotland."

Their own cabin! Boris wondered if they would have beds. Or maybe hammocks?

Their friend Sir Luther Fangdolph met them on the platform. Sir Luther was a well-connected wolf with an interest in Wolfish history. He'd been getting the Greycoats' travel documents in order.

"Did you know, you are the first wolves to be reintroduced to Scotland!" announced Sir Luther, as he handed Leonora two passports. "The Scots Conservation Society is terribly excited."

"Ah well, that was to be expected," said Randall, looking pleased. Sir Luther smiled down at Boris. "Your passport, Boris dear."

Boris's cub passport had a Morovian crest on the front. Inside, there was a picture of Boris (with his ears slicked back and his whiskers trimmed). And something new and shiny on the page opposite.

"That's your Scottish visa, with the new Lupine insignia," said Sir Luther. "It's been designed especially for us wolves."

Boris stared at the silver visa sticker, with its wiggly patterns

and loopy writing. If you squinted a bit you could see a thistle, a paw mark and what could be feathers– or maybe just squiggles.

"The train's boarding!" said Sir Luther. "You'd better get on. Goodbye! And remember to make a good impression!"

"Thank you," said Boris, "I'll try."

He put the fancy passport in his pocket, heaved his rucksack onto his back (*The History of the Scottish Greycoats* was heavy) and followed his parents onto the train.

To ensure a comfortable journey, the wolves decided to eat first. As the train left the station, they settled down to an early lunch in the Emperor of Prussia dining carriage.

"I'll have the shrimp bavarois to start with," said Leonora to the waiter. "And the venison to follow. And for you, Randall dearest?"

"Mmm," said Randall, "I'll make do with the truffle poached eggs …

"And the leg of lamb," he added, licking his chops. "Boris?"

Boris was distracted. Two well-dressed ladies at the next table were staring at them. One was frowning at Randall, her lips pursed disapprovingly. The other lady was nervously clutching her handbag.

Leonora had noticed their distress. To ease their anxiety, she gave the ladies one of her warm, reassuring smiles.

Maybe it was the way Leonora's teeth popped out to the side, or the way her upper lip curled, but the ladies did not seem reassured. The nervous lady grabbed her handbag and hurried out of the carriage. The other lady tutted. "Wolves in first class!" she said loudly. She gathered her fur shawl, tossed it round her neck and got up. "Disgraceful!" she added as she swept past.

Leonora raised an eyebrow and looked toward Randall, who was engrossed in the dessert menu.

Boris scowled at the lady. How dare she!

The lady pushed past the waiter and turned to glare at the wolves, not seeing Boris's bag, which had tipped over into the aisle.

"Ow!" said the lady, as she stubbed her toe on

The History of the Scottish Greycoats by Baron McLupus the Fifteenth. Red-faced, she hopped up and down, and her fur shawl came loose.

Nearby, an elderly gentleman was tucking into a big bowl of pea soup. The fur fell in.

"My mink!" the lady shrieked.

"Hoy!" cried the man. "There's hair in my soup!"

The lady snatched the fur away, spattering thick green soup over the poor gentleman.

"Now there's soup in my hair!" he said miserably.

"They started it!" the lady screeched, pointing at the wolves. She hobbled out of the carriage and slammed the door.

"Serves her right," whispered Boris to his mother.

"Be polite, Boris!" said Leonora. But Boris thought he saw her suppress a smile.

Some staff came to help the man, and Boris checked the menu. Their waiter was getting impatient. He clicked his pen and tutted.

"Perhaps some chicken nuggets for the …" the waiter looked at Boris, "… cub?"

Chicken nuggets! No way! This was a vacation and Boris wanted something fancy.

"I'll have the whisky-soaked prawns, please," he told the waiter, "then the brandy chicken."

The waiter stared.

"But leave out the whisky and brandy, of course," added Boris.

The waiter frowned and made a note.

"Is there cake?" asked Boris.

"The correct term is *dessert*," said the waiter. He pointed at the menu. "Dessert includes cakes."

Boris was fond of cake.

"Oh, good!" he said. "Then I'll have a cream scone, a piece of pear flan and a chocolate eclair.

That's three desserts, please!

"To use the correct term," he added, to be polite.

Extract from *A Guide to Morovia*

by Brydie Phelan

Wolves have been part of Morovian life for centuries. Wolves and humans mingle comfortably on Morovia's cobbled streets, when dining out, at the ballet and on the ski slopes.

However, wolves may discover less relaxed attitudes abroad. For example, most traveling Morovian wolves avoid foreign countryside for fear of attacks by farmers. Instead, wolf tourists prefer historic cities, where they can take in the cultural sights.

Even in Morovia, some humans look down on wolves as "ill-mannered" or "uncultured."

In fact, most Morovian wolves have excellent manners. Cubs are taught from a young age to be graceful when confronted by rudeness.

Which doesn't mean they have to put up with just anything, of course.

After a long, delicious lunch, followed by a game of wolf scrabble and a light, tasty supper, the Greycoat family retired to their private quarters.

Boris was entranced by the cozy, wood-paneled sleeping compartment. By one window were the beds—a single bunk up high and a double bunk down below. A foil-wrapped candy lay on each of the pillows. By the other window were two curved, padded sofas. There were lamps in nooks that gave off warm light, clever shelves that folded out of the walls, and soft velvet curtains around the beds. There was even a little sink with gold taps.

It was perfect luxury. Boris stashed his candy and snuggled into one of the sofas by the window. While Randall trimmed his whiskers and Leonora perched on the bed to write in her diary, Boris watched houses, then forests, then mountains flit past in the evening light.

Soon it was dark outside. Boris unwrapped his candy. It was a sugared chestnut and surprisingly delicious. He flattened the foil wrapper and stuck it inside his sketchbook. Then he climbed up into his bunk and

got out *The History of the Scottish Greycoats.*

It was an entertaining read, full of dramatic stories from hundreds of years ago. Boris read about Lambert McLupus, the first wolf to become a Scottish baron. Lambert looked very proud in front of his castle, Wolfemina Hall, in the middle of a Scottish glen.

But the Baron had enemies. His treacherous brothers, Lyall and Lowell McLupus, plotted to take Wolfemina Hall for themselves.

LYALL

LOWELL

They sneaked into the Hall and hid in suits of armor, planning to attack at midnight. But the wicked wolves got stuck in their armor. They wandered onto a balcony, tripped, and fell to their doom in the castle moat.

According to the book, the ghosts of the two brothers then spitefully haunted Lambert McLupus for the rest of his life.

LYALL (or possibly Lowell)

LOWELL (or possibly Lyall)

How mean of them! thought Boris. It wasn't *Lambert's* fault they fell in the moat.

As he brushed his fangs, Boris was suddenly very sleepy. He snuggled under the covers and, despite the spooky tale he'd just read, Boris dozed off, dreaming of castles, romantic glens and chocolate eclairs.

CHAPTER 3

By Land, Sea and Land

Boris woke to the smell of fresh baking. It was morning, and there was a pile of hot, buttered croissants on the little table by the window.

"Yum!" said Boris cheerfully. He put on his fluffy dressing gown, sat down and tucked in.

Then he looked out the window. The train was stopped on the platform!

"Dad!" said Boris. "We've stopped! And it says 'Rotterdam'! Don't we need to get off?"

"Don't worry," said Randall, looking up from his book, *Learn Scots in 30 Days*.

"Your mother had a chat with the train staff and we can stay on board for an hour or so. Our ferry doesn't leave Rotterdam Port till the afternoon, you see."

Outside, on the platform, the rude lady from the restaurant was arguing with one of the train porters. Boris pricked up his ears. He did like to hear what people were saying.

"I'm sorry, ma'am," the porter was explaining, "but everyone must disembark at Rotterdam."

"But I hadn't finished my breakfast!" said the lady, indignantly. "And that carriage is still occupied!" She pointed at Boris.

"Certainly, ma'am. But those people have made arrangements."

"People? They're *wolves*!"

The lady glared at Boris. Boris would have loved to press his snout up to the glass, cross his eyes and make a face. But he had been taught to be polite in public.

So, instead, Boris grinned at the lady and slowly took a huge bite of his lovely, flaky croissant. Then he settled back in his chair, making it plain that he was extra comfy in his carriage.

The lady's mouth fell open. She picked up her bags and stalked off down the platform.

"Are you finished, sir?" It was the waiter from last night.

"Mph hmph!" said Boris, his mouth still full of croissant. The waiter raised his eyebrows.

"Apologies," said Boris, "but these croissants are delicious! Do you have the recipe? I've had croissants in Morovia, but for some reason they didn't taste nice at all."

MOROVIAN CROISSANTS
NOT FOR EATING
GOOD FOR BOOMERANGS

"Up at last, Boris!" said Leonora, as Boris wrote down the last of the croissant recipe.

Croissants were fiddly to make, the waiter had told him. *But worth it*, thought Boris.

"Feet a baw nee owled stain," said Randall, suddenly.

Boris and Leonora stared.

"What?" said Boris.

"Pardon?" said Leonora.

"I said 'what a stunning standing stone,'" replied Randall, "in Scots. One of the native tongues of the Scottish people. I want to make sure we blend in."

Boris wondered how his father, a large wolf wearing glasses and tweed trousers and reading Scots loudly from a phrase book, was going to blend in. So far, on their family vacations, the wolves had mostly attracted attention, and not always in a good way.

"How wonderful, darling," said Leonora, "but I think most people in Scotland can speak English …"

"Mmm," said Randall, "maybe so, but I do have a gift for languages. And I've been learning Scots since Tuesday. I can't let all that effort go to waste."

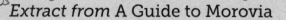

Extract from A Guide to Morovia

by Brydie Phelan

ENGLISH: AT HOME	FRENCH: EATING OUT	PRUSSIAN: ASSERTIVE
CAN YOU FETCH MORE BREAD, DEAR?	DU PAIN, S'IL VOUS PLAIT *	NUSAN DENIMAN GEITIN BROE! *
	* SOME BREAD, PLEASE	* GIVE ME BREAD!

The wolves of Morovia's native tongue is, of course, Morovian. But most cultured wolves speak English at home and in conversation, French while dining out, and Medieval Prussian when asserting themselves.

As a young Morovian wolf, Boris already knew four languages. And his father spoke many more. As well as being a polymath, Randall was also a polyglot, which is someone who can speak lots of languages.

Sometimes though, Boris wondered if Randall was saying the *right* things in all of these languages.

Finally, after a late lunch, the wolves left their comfortable cabin and disembarked the train.

They spent the afternoon wandering around the Port of Rotterdam and looking at a lot of ships and bridges. Then it was time to take the ferry.

While some people drove their cars onto the ferry, the wolves lined up on foot. Boris couldn't wait to show off his new passport.

"Very nice," said the ticket inspector, "but I need a ticket and this is a passport, although it is very nice."

"Oh," said Boris, "my parents have the tickets. Do you like the Lupine insignia?"

"Most unusual," said the inspector. "Traveling wolves! And what is that book?"

"It's our family history," said Boris, holding out *The History of the Scottish Greycoats* by Baron McLupus the Fifteenth.

"Wonderful!" said the inspector. "I must find myself a copy. Have a good trip, little cub!"

Boris decided he liked Dutch ticket inspectors.

The ferry was like an enormous floating hotel, with lots of corridors and stairs and comfy places to sit. The wolves went down to their "deluxe" cabin. It was cozy, warmly lit and had bunks in every corner. There were two round portholes and–Boris was delighted to see–each bunk had a gold-wrapped Swiss chocolate on the pillow.

Boris tried all the bunks. He bounced, then he lay down and rolled on each one. Finally he decided on the bunk with a porthole at the foot end. Boris waggled his hind paws and watched the waves slosh against the thick glass. He decided to save his chocolate for later.

They had a fascinating time wandering the deck– Boris counted thirty-two flights of stairs. There were heavy banging doors that went outside and storm warnings on the walls, and flashing machines with exciting things to buy inside. Boris was taken by an arcade machine with a huge stuffed shark inside.

"Even if you did win, it wouldn't fit in your backpack," said Randall. "Let's go to the cinema."

After an exciting superhero movie and a bucket of popcorn the wolves settled in their sleeping quarters.

I wonder what it would be like to spend every night in a different cabin, thought Boris, tucking the cinema ticket into his notebook. He decided it would be marvelous. Rocked by the waves and still clutching his gold-wrapped chocolate, he went to sleep.

The next morning the ferry arrived in Hull, England. The wolves were in a hurry to get to the train station. But each time a cab pulled up to the front of the stand and saw the wolves, the driver would move on.

"They must be confused," said Randall.

"Or maybe this is the back of the line?" said Leonora.

"Humph!" said Boris. It was cold and drizzly and he hadn't had time to finish his breakfast. As soon as the next taxi pulled up, he flung open the door to the back seat and sat down. If this taxi driver was scared of wolves, she could just deal with it.

He beckoned his parents in.

Boris smiled at the driver, being careful not to show his fangs. He gave her his gold-wrapped chocolate

because it seemed a nice thing to do. It was only slightly squished.

"The train station, please, and quickly. We're on our way to Scotland!" he said, feeling a sudden thrill. Scotland! At last!

They arrived at the station just in time for the train. Boris and Randall hastily unloaded their bags as Leonora paid the fare. Boris turned to wave as they dashed toward the platform and the driver waved back. He noticed she was nibbling the chocolate.

The train to Scotland didn't have cabins. They sat at a table in a busy carriage. Everyone was concentrating on their newspapers or fiddling with phones and computers, and no one seemed to notice the wolves. Feeling relaxed, Boris rested his snout on the glass and watched the English countryside whizz by.

"Ah," said Randall a couple of hours later, "we're crossing the border. I can feel the blood of my ancestors stirring within. We're coming home at last!"

And Scotland did look different. The light was soft, the hills were purple and the buildings looked gray and solid in a comforting sort of way.

"How are you getting on with our ancestors, Boris?" asked Leonora. "I'd love to know what you're learning about the McLupus family."

Boris pulled *The History of the Scottish Greycoats* out of his backpack.

"I'm not too far in yet," he said, "but I'll tell you after the next chapter."

He opened the book and started to read. What had happened to Baron Lambert McLupus after his brothers fell in the moat?

It turned out that Lambert McLupus, the first baron of Wolfemina Hall, had three sons–Romulus, Remus and Rufus. Romulus was the oldest (though not by much as they were triplets), so he was in line to inherit Wolfemina Hall. But, like their uncles before them, Remus and Rufus were jealous of the heir to the title.

Romulus, Remus and Rufus McLupus

In fact, all three sons were bitter rivals. Each brother spent his life trying to get rid of the other two brothers. Finally, one day, after attempting to trip Romulus with a rope, Remus slipped and fell off a mountain. Romulus celebrated the incident with a bottle of mead, forgetting that he'd poisoned the mead earlier when planning to gift it to Remus.

Romulus gloating over a glass of mead

Romulus choking over a glass of mead

How wicked! thought Boris. *Serves him right!*

And so Rufus, the surviving triplet, inherited Wolfemina Hall, becoming the second Baron McLupus.

Rufus McLupus at Wolfemina Hall

Boris thought Rufus looked smug. Or relieved. It was hard to tell.

CHAPTER 4

Gateway to the Highlands

"We're here! We're here!" said Randall.

It seemed the people of Inverness hadn't seen a family of wolves step off a train before. Everyone was looking at them curiously.

Just then, a lady walked toward them.

"Welcome to Scotland!" she said. "I'm Aileen Fordyce from the Scottish Royal Conservation Society. Scots Conservation for short."

Aileen was dressed in loose trousers and a large, woolly shawl. She had a lovely big nose. Wolves like people with big noses. Big noses are a sign of good character.

"Madame Fordyce! *Enchanté**!" said Randall, taking her hand in his paw and kissing it.

Aileen Fordyce blushed. She was clearly thrilled to see them.

"This is my wife, Leonora, and our son, Boris," said Randall.

"Delighted!" said Leonora, kissing Aileen on each cheek.

"Where will you be staying?" Aileen asked. "I can help you find a nice spot in the forest if you wish."

Leonora gave Aileen Fordyce one of her warmest and most reassuring smiles.

"My dear, we would love to weekend in a forest lodge," she said, "but for now we're taking rooms at the Highland Hotel—until we get ourselves settled."

"The Highland!" said Aileen. She seemed surprised. The Highland was probably a fancy hotel, Boris realized. Maybe Aileen Fordyce had expected something different.

---

* ("*Enchanté*" is French for "enchanted." Wolves and French people might say this when they meet people.)

"Our friend Sir Luther has organized a chauffeur to take us there after lunch," said Randall. "Shall we dine together first?"

"Oh, my! Lunch would be lovely," said Aileen Fordyce. "There's the Railway Inn, just next door."

"Wonderful," said Leonora. She took Aileen's arm and, bags in paws, the wolves went to lunch.

At the Railway Inn, Randall ordered a ploughman's lunch with a leg of ham on the side. Boris and Leonora had prawns, and Aileen ordered turnip soup.

"So most Scots know that wolves are being reintroduced," said Aileen Fordyce, "but I'm not sure they'll expect you to be staying at the Highland Hotel."

She tucked into her soup. "And it may take a while for the local people to get used to you. The sheep farmers are worried …"

"Oh, we won't take up farming," said Leonora.

"Ha ha, no!" said Aileen. Boris could see that she thought Leonora was joking.

"Though," said Randall, "if we were to farm, we could grow barley, perhaps."

Aileen Fordyce seemed less sure they were joking now.

She turned to Boris. "Do you have any questions about Scotland?"

"Boris has been reading up on our ancestors," said Randall, proudly.

This made Boris a bit shy, but he did have a question.

"Do you know about a castle called Wolfemina Hall?" he asked. "The McLupuses lived there hundreds of years ago.

"They were wolves," he added, thinking that might be important.

Aileen stared at him. "I don't. But I'd love to know more."

"Just out of interest," said Leonora, "can wolves buy property in Scotland?"

"We thought we might buy a vacation home, you see," explained Randall.

Boris looked at Aileen. It was clear she hadn't expected any of this.

Leonora was sensitive to the feelings of others. She patted Aileen on the arm.

"Maybe we can talk about this another time," she said. "Would you like dessert? Lunch is on us. It's so lovely to meet you."

"Of course … *C'est pour nous!**" said Randall, speaking French for the second time that day. Boris wished he wouldn't. It was embarrassing.

---

* "*C'est pour nous*" is French for "it's for us," which means "we will pay for this." Most wolves are generous and enjoy treating their friends to fancy meals.

After dessert, an antique car pulled up outside the Railway Inn to take the wolves to their hotel.

"What a lovely old Bentley," said Leonora.

Just then, a stocky man in a green tweed suit ran out of the station. He barged past, knocking *The History of the Scottish Greycoats* out of Boris's paws.

"Well," said Aileen Fordyce, "how rude!" She picked up Boris's book.

"Is this the book about your ancestors?" she asked. "Fascinating! I must get a copy for our library. Take care of it!"

As Aileen and his parents made arrangements to keep in touch, Boris heard the man in the green tweed arguing with the driver of the car.

"What do you mean?" said the man. "This is the Highland Hotel car, isn't it? So take me to the Highland Hotel!"

Leonora went over to the car. She popped her luggage down beside the man and cleared her throat.

"Do pop these in the trunk, kind sir," she said to him. "I'll keep my handbag with me."

The man whirled around to see a large, female

wolf standing right next to him. It didn't help that Leonora had her pearls on and was carrying a handbag. Or that Randall, dressed in a checkered waistcoat and breeches, was making his way back to the car, walking rather briskly and rubbing his paws together. Or that a small wolf was glaring at him, and clutching an enormous book. Just then, the man forgot to be angry. He gawped. And Boris got a good look at his face.

It wasn't a friendly face. The man's eyes had a beady, greedy look to them.

I wouldn't leave him alone with a roast boar, thought Boris. *Not to be trusted.*

Leonora gave the man her best warm, reassuring smile. At least two of her fangs popped out the side. Terrified, the man took hold of their suitcases and loaded them into the trunk of the car. This was a good thing, as the chauffeur had realized his passengers were to be wolves. Instead of helping with the baggage, he was sitting in the driver's seat, gripping the steering wheel and staring straight ahead.

Aileen Fordyce helped Boris into the car.

"It may take a little while for people to get used to you," she said, "but you'll be fine."

She smiled brightly at the man in green tweed. "Oh, hello, Mr. Vorslad," she said. "You'll have to get a taxi today, I'm afraid."

By this time the man was red in the face and clearly furious.

"But you've been terribly helpful!" Randall said breezily. "Do take a little extra something, my dear sir. *Noblesse oblige**!" And he offered Mr. Vorslad a crisp twenty-pound note.

Speechless, Mr. Vorslad just glared at Randall's money. Then he grabbed his bags and stormed off toward the taxi stand, giving them all a nasty look over his shoulder.

"Green tweed! Interesting outfits the Scottish porters have," commented Leonora, as they settled into the back seat.

---

* *"Noblesse oblige"* is French for "The noble ones ought to pay." It means that if you're wealthier than other people, you should be honorable and generous toward them.

"The Highland Hotel, my dear man," said Randall, and off they went, waving to the lovely Aileen Fordyce as they left.

Their chauffeur was nervous of the wolves at first. But then Leonora told him about their old Bentley back in Morovia, Randall shared his knowledge of Jacobites and Boris shared his caramels. The chauffeur relaxed. His name was Jim and he was full of facts on the area, as well as on the hotel guests.

The antique car reminded Boris of the train. It had lots of useful places to pull things out of and put things down on. Boris pulled out a tiny can of ginger ale, opened it, and put it down on a shelf in the door. Three ginger ales (and five caramels) later, they arrived at the hotel driveway.

The Highland Hotel sat near a cliff top, overlooking the sea. It was a sprawling building of glittering gray stone. The design of the hotel was vastly elaborate, with lots of pointy windows and roofs, jutting chimneys and battlements, balustrades and towers added for good measure.

"Victorian," said Randall, knowledgeably.

"It's a bit of a monstrosity," said Jim.

"Of course the Highland Hotel is famous these days," said Jim. "Lots of successful people come here to stay. Pop stars, actors, politicians …"

A taxi, which had been close behind the Bentley for the whole journey, pulled past them suddenly and came to an abrupt halt right in front of the hotel, blocking their way. Mr. Vorslad got out of the taxi. He made a point of striding haughtily toward the hotel entrance, nose in the air.

"… and property developers," said the chauffeur, frowning.

Boris thought the Highland Hotel was just magical. It was completely different than the buildings in Morovia. It looked like something out of a storybook.

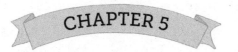

CHAPTER 5

Discovering a Castle

In the foyer a whiskery black dog with short, stubby legs rushed at their ankles, barking gruffly.

"Hamish," said the receptionist, "lie down!"

With a warning growl, Hamish trotted over to a red velvet cushion. He lay down, eyeing the wolves with suspicion.

If the receptionist was surprised to see wolves, she didn't show it.

"Welcome, Mr., Mrs. and Master Greycoat," she said. "You're in the Jacobite suite. And don't mind Hamish. He thinks he runs the place."

The first thing Boris noticed about the Jacobite

suite was the carpet. It was a bright red-and-gold tartan pattern and the same in every room. The second thing he noticed was that the curtains and the bedspreads, and even the towels, were all in matching tartan.

Maybe all Scottish houses have tartan curtains and beds and floors, thought Boris.

Two huge arched windows looked onto the beach, a long crescent of golden sand. Beyond was the sea, dark blue and choppy.

Hamish had tailed them upstairs. He hauled himself up onto a window seat and growled at a gull flying past.

The wolves organized their suitcases and set off to explore. It was brisk weather, so Randall wore his tweed jacket and a sheepskin hat with ear flaps. Boris was forced by Leonora to wear a beanie and scarf.

"Where shall we go first?" asked Boris, clutching the map the receptionist had given him.

Randall grabbed his binoculars and peered down the hill. "Come along, all!" he said. "I may have spotted a rare speckled lapwing!"

Oh no, thought Boris. *Bird-watching!*

Boris was sort of interested in birds, if they were exciting birds like eagles or puffins. But right now he was interested in beaches and exploring. Bird-watching meant being bored stiff while Randall and Leonora looked through binoculars and said things like: "Look, darling, a spotted tern!"

Boris looked for interesting places to distract his mum and dad with.

At the Highland Hotel end of the beach were dunes, crags and huge, cathedral-like rocks. On the other end, further away, there was a harbor, a pretty-looking seaside village and some woods, which swept up from the sands to the top of a steep hill.

And then Boris saw it …

"Mum! Dad! There's a Scottish castle!"

By the top of the hill, a couple of turrets and some battlements poked out from the trees.

Like many Morovian wolves, Boris was fascinated by castles, and so were his parents. The Greycoats also loved turrets, which is why Greycoat Hall had twenty-three of them. The Greycoat family even had a turret motto: "Always enough and never too many."

Recommended use of turrets in Morovia

"It must be this one!" said Randall, checking the map. "Ah, yes … Drommuir Castle! Well, I think we should have a look."

So, following the map, they walked down to the beach and along the sand, with Randall and Leonora stopping to spot birds on the way. After they'd spotted petrels, oystercatchers and a hundred gulls, Boris was relieved to see some wooden steps leading to the hill.

"This way!" he said.

There was a large placard by the steps. It read: *Protect our wildlife! Protect our castle! Say NO to Vorslad Villas!*

At the top of the steps, two paths led into the forest. The path on the left was signposted *Drommuir Castle–steep but short path.* The sign for the other path said, *Drommuir Castle–gentle but long path.*

They decided on "steep but short path."

Maybe it's a ruined, spooky castle! thought Boris, as he puffed his way up the hill.

"Wait!" said Randall. "There's something in the bushes! It could be a rare speckled lapwing. Where's my bird book?"

As Randall studied *The Guide to the Birds of Scotland*, a huge rumpus started up in the bush near Boris. Boris took a few steps back. He hoped Scotland didn't have bears—or lions.

The bush snorted.

Randall was still studying his book, muttering about rare species.

Suddenly a huge, hairy creature lunged at Boris.

"Aaaaaagh!" yelled Boris and Leonora.

"Aroooooo!" said the shape. "Woof!"

It was a shaggy dog with long, spindly legs.

"Hello!" said Boris, delighted. "Where did you come from?"

The dog barked cheerfully. She licked his snout.

"It can't be a lapwing!" said Randall, still studying his book. "They nest in the dunes, not bushes. Good to have expert knowledge on these things."

He didn't appear to have noticed the dog at all. Book in hand, he strode up the hill.

Boris and Leonora grinned at each other. They followed on, the shaggy dog panting at their heels.

After a rugged climb, the wolves and the dog arrived at the castle.

Boris gasped.

"Gosh," said Leonora, "it's perfect!"

Drommuir Castle looked just like a Scottish castle should. Surrounded by grand and stately trees, it was fierce and strong looking, but friendly too. There were three turrets and three solid, stepped chimneys, a bell tower and a balcony with proper Scottish battlements.

But the castle also looked slightly shabby, as

though no one had lived there for a while. It needed painting, and there were slates missing from the roof.

The wolves read a sign by the front drive: *Currently closed to the public.*

Another sign was propped in the middle of the driveway. It said: *Say YES to Vorslad Villas! Much better than a drafty old castle!*

"It's a wonderful castle. Who cares if it's drafty?" said Leonora, looking puzzled.

Randall rushed ahead and started peering into the windows.

"Fascinating interior," he called to them. "Shame we can't get in."

There was a carving by the front door. Boris was surprised to see it looked like a wolf's paw. He got out his sketchbook, placed a page over the carving and rubbed with his extra-thick black pencil until the shape of the carving came through on the paper.

SAY
YES
to
VORSLAD
VILLAS!

The dog bounded ahead. She barked at them. "Come along!" she was saying. Boris followed her behind a tall hedge to a garden full of raspberries. Disappointingly, the berries weren't ripe, though Boris supposed he shouldn't eat them anyway.

They came to a walled garden. In the middle was a miniature stone castle with turrets. It was the size of a tiny cottage. There was just one room inside, with stairs up to a balcony.

"Aha! A folly," declared Randall. "An ornamental building, with no practical purpose," he explained to Boris.

"It's adorable!" said Leonora.

The dog plonked herself down in a corner.

Maybe this is where she sleeps, thought Boris, as he rubbed her belly.

"Is that a grouse?" said Randall. He got out his binoculars and soon he and Leonora were spotting birds in the garden trees.

Boris sighed. He got out his bag and sat in a rock garden, sketching the folly. Perhaps he could build a miniature castle back home at Greycoat Hall.

"Honk!" Boris jumped. A huge blue and green peacock was staring at him haughtily.

"Grrrr," said the dog and the peacock strutted away. It reminded Boris of the snooty lady on the train.

He giggled. His parents were still peering through their binoculars looking for birds. And a huge peacock was only a few feet away!

As they wandered back to the castle, the wolves crossed a little stone bridge over a grassy ditch.

"Why's there a bridge?" asked Boris. "There's no water."

"Aha," said Randall, "I expect Drommuir had an ornamental moat. Long ago, it would have been surrounded by water."

"Not enough to keep enemies out," explained Leonora, "but just a small moat, for looks."

The dog settled down on the front step. "Bye for now," said Boris, "and be kind to the peacock."

The dog watched them as they headed down the "gentle but long" path.

Boris wondered who she belonged to.

CHAPTER 6

Fish in the Air

By now, the wolves were very, very hungry.

As all respectable wolves know, the best way to get on in society is to *not* get very, very hungry. A hungry wolf is not a dignified wolf.

Leonora sensibly insisted they go to the village to find food.

Soon the wolves came to the village harbor. A delightfully fishy smell wafted past their snouts. To Boris's joy, there was a shop nearby, with a sign saying *BUY FISH HERE!*

"I shall enquire within," said Randall, licking his chops. So Boris and Leonora sat on a little bench by the thick seawall and, tummies rumbling, waited for their fish.

A few minutes later, Randall came out of the shop. There was no paper package in his paws. In fact, there was nothing at all.

"Didn't they have fish?" asked Leonora, in her very politest tone.

Randall stood there, his tail drooping.

"Um. Lots of fish," said Randall. "Darling … what language do they speak in these parts?"

"They might speak Gaelic," said Leonora, "but most Scottish people speak English or Scots."

"Oh …" said Randall.

"Let's go in, all of us," said Leonora, briskly. Boris realized his mother was as hungry as he was.

Extract from A Guide to Morovia
by Brydie Phelan

Although the wolves of Morovia are sophisticated, thoughtful and, above all, polite, they possess powerful appetites.

As a precaution, a wolf must not appear in society when hungry—as this hunger may result in Undignified Situations and Embarrassing Incidents.

EMBARRASSING INCIDENT | UNDIGNIFIED SITUATION

While Morovian wolves prefer their food cooked, arranged nicely and served on a plate with a variety of condiments and relishes, they will also eat whatever they can get their paws on, including:

★ Shells and bones
★ Wrapping paper
★ Bananas including peel
★ Raw eggs including cardboard carton
★ Butter directly from package

* Month-old Bolognese sauce
* Slow-moving rodents
* Leather slippers

Things that a wolf may not eat, or will prefer not to eat, are listed below:

* Dark chocolate (if more than six bars)
* Carrots

BEFORE HUNGRY WOLF | AFTER HUNGRY WOLF

A friendly man in a stripy apron grinned at them from behind a counter of fresh-looking fish.

"Good afternoon," said Leonora. And she gave the fishmonger her warmest reassuring smile.

The fishmonger kept grinning. He nodded toward the fish.

"Ayeyoolbe lookinferfish wulyenae?" he said.

The wolves stared. Leonora made her smile warmer still. A couple more of her teeth popped out the side. But the fishmonger didn't seem to mind.

He said, "Oorcoods ahfaydeer. Butahcan dee sumscallops fertenpoon?"

He pointed at a tray of fresh scallops.

"So sorry to hear," said Randall, backing out of the shop. Nodding and smiling, he tugged at Boris's scarf.

"Let's go," he hissed, "the man is clearly confused."

Boris was looking at the tasty scallops, his mouth watering. *No way!* he thought. *We need food!*

"Mum!" said Boris, urgently. "I can do this. Just give me some money."

Quickly Leonora handed Boris several large notes. The fishmonger raised his eyebrows, looking hopeful.

Boris laid the money on the counter.

"Your fish looks very good!" he said slowly and clearly. Then Boris decided to speak normally.

He had a feeling the fishmonger could understand them perfectly well.

"We'll have whatever you think is tasty," he said, pointing at the money, "up to this amount."

The fishmonger grinned even more broadly. He started bagging up all the shellfish, a dozen whole fish, and a mound of tasty-looking fillets.

"Wullye winta bittachange?" he asked, handing over several large paper parcels.

"Yes, certainly, lovely day to you too!" said Randall, more cheerfully now, pulling them all out the door.

"I haven't quite worked out his ethnic tongue," he whispered to Boris, "but it may be Basque, or perhaps ... Pictish ..."

"Possibly, Dad," said Boris.

Hungrier than they thought possible, the wolves sat on a bench by the harbor and guzzled every bit of fish, including the shells, and most of the wrapping paper as well.

"Maybe," said Boris, once the last fillet had gone, "that's just how some Scottish people talk."

"Help!" said Leonora. "How will we get by?"

She smiled and waved at an elderly couple on a nearby bench. The couple got up hastily and made off toward the village. Boris wondered if they'd been watching the wolves eat. He hoped not.

CHAPTER 7

Tea and Tartan

The next morning was bright and sunny. Boris ate up his porridge, kippers and oatcakes. Out the window, gulls squawked and waves crashed.

Boris cleaned his whiskers and packed his caramels, notebook and plastic shovel. Then, trying to be patient, he waited while Randall finished the business section of the newspaper and Leonora sipped her second cup of tea.

"All right, let's go," he said.

The wolves decided to explore the village past the harbor. The tide was in and there was no sand this time. So they had to hop and jump over rocks.

Boris pretended he was a mountain goat. Then he pretended to be a giant leaping over rivers and valleys. Then he noticed his parents were staring through their binoculars again.

Oh, please, thought Boris. *No more bird-watching!*

"Come and see," called Randall.

Out to sea were some lumpy black rocks. Boris squinted through the binoculars. The rocks were moving.

SEALS - viewed from the shore

"They're seals," said Leonora. "And there are dolphins further out too."

DOLPHINS - viewed from the shore

His parents spotted more lumpy black things, and more rocks.

ROCKS - viewed from the shore

"Please can we go to the village now?" said Boris, trying not to whine. The seals weren't getting any nearer and some of them actually were rocks.

On the way to the village they saw more *No to Vorslad Villas!* signs, as well as *Protect our seabirds and dolphins!*, *Protect our otters!*, *Stop the development –for the sake of our seals!*

These villas are bad news, thought Boris. *For the animals, anyway.*

The village was called Portlessie. It overlooked the harbor and a little bay. It had gift shops, antique shops, a supermarket, a few officey-looking buildings and a café called Tea by the Sea, with an ice cream sign outside.

The wolves decided to potter along the street and look in the shops. Unfortunately Jim the chauffeur had told Leonora about all the village antique shops, and she was keen to see them for herself.

Antiques, thought Boris, *yuck!* He couldn't understand what was so interesting about a few old jugs and lamps and candlesticks.

"Oh look, darling," his mother was saying to Randall, "an Edwardian spoon!"

At last, after six antique shops, they were nearly at the end of the street.

"Randall!" said Leonora, pointing to a notice in a real estate office.

Boris sighed. Looking at house prices was even worse than antiques or bird-watching. Vacations were supposed to be fun. What was wrong with his parents?

Boris's tummy rumbled and he looked longingly at Tea by the Sea, just a few shops away. "Mum, Dad … can I get something from the café?"

"Of course … of course …" said his father, sounding distracted.

Leonora handed Boris a twenty-pound note. "Good idea. Can you get a couple of scones for us too, to keep us all going?"

The tea shop was nearly empty except for one customer. By the counter stood the man in the green tweed suit.

"YOU!" he said angrily as Boris came in. He turned to the tea shop lady.

"This is the last straw, Mrs. McKay! You vote against my villas, you put up ridiculous signs and now you let *animals* into your shop! Good day to you!" And he left, slamming the door behind him.

"And good riddance!" said Mrs. McKay, the café lady. She looked warily at Boris. She probably hadn't seen a wolf before, Boris realized. He tried to look extra friendly. It was important to introduce oneself politely.

"Your very good Scottish morning," he said. "Can I have three scones, please?"

He glanced at the fabulous array of cakes by the counter. "And maybe one of those pancakes with jam. And a chocolate eclair. Hang on!"

He dashed outside. His parents were entering a touristy tartan shop called "Check us Oot." They were bound to take ages.

"And some tea, please? Can you put the scones in a bag? And I'll have the rest here."

Mrs. McKay showed Boris to a window seat.

Nearby, sat a lady with two young children. The older boy pointed at Boris, so he waved to him. But the lady looked alarmed. She pulled her small girl onto her knee.

An elderly couple at another table were watching Boris anxiously. He recognized them as the couple from the harbor yesterday.

Oh no, thought Boris, *they* did *see us gobble up the fish.*

Today, he would eat his cakes delicately.

Just then, Jim the chauffeur came into the shop.

"Hello, young Greycoat!" he said to Boris. "Mind if I join you?"

"Please do!" said Boris.

Jim sat down. He placed a shiny document on the table.

"What's that?" asked Boris.

"It's the sales brochure for Vorslad Villas," said Mrs. McKay, arriving with a tray. "Just take a look!"

The front of the brochure showed a tall, shiny tower surrounded by apartment buildings. Boris read the text inside:

LUXURY VACATION VILLAS

–by the forest and the sea.

Enjoy hunting, shooting, puffin collecting, seal herding, dolphin racing, jet-skiing and salmon blasting! Spend your money at the sky-high revolving restaurant!

"Salmon blasting?" said Boris. "How horrible! So Vorslad Villas must belong to Mr. Vorslad!" Now Boris disliked him even more.

"It does. And it's a disaster!" said Jim.

"And that Vorslad wants me to take down my petition!" said Mrs. McKay, pointing to a long list of names on the wall, under the heading "Say NO to Vorslad Villas."

"I'll sign it," said Boris. He got up and wrote his full name, Boris Fenrir Wolfgang McLupus Greycoat, at the bottom of the list, then added "DISGRACEFUL!!!" next to it.

"Thank you, dear," said Mrs. McKay, smiling.

Jim ordered tea and carrot cake.

"Do you have tartan carpet at home," Boris asked him, "and tartan curtains?"

Jim roared with laughter. "Not all Scottish houses look like the Highland Hotel," he said. "That's just for the tourists."

Over tea, Jim told Boris about the hotel guests. That week, a film star had asked for an otter to be brought to her room.

"We drew the line at that one!" said Jim.

A businessman had arrived by helicopter just after breakfast that morning, making an "unbelievable racket." And Mr. Vorslad was one of the hotel's most demanding guests. He insisted on the McBride suite whenever he stayed, and expected black pudding and sausages in his room at five every morning.

"And for some reason, he particularly hates dogs," Jim told Boris. "We try to keep Hamish away, but the wee fellow always gets into Mr. Vorslad's room. He ran off with Mr. Vorslad's slippers this morning."

He sniggered to himself.

"Anyway, I should go. Lots to do! Have fun today."

He paid Mrs. McKay and headed down the street, waving cheerfully at Boris.

"I was wondering," said Boris, as he paid for his cakes, "what were those pancakes? The ones with jam and cream. They were delicious!"

Mrs. McKay smiled. "They're Bannocks! Named after the Battle of Bannockburn. They're awfully easy to make. Would you like the recipe?"

"Yes, please!" said Boris.

Boris got out his notebook and pen. The recipe did seem simple.

"What's baking soda?" asked Boris.

"It's a leavening agent," said Mrs. McKay. "It helps make cakes light and fluffy."

"Mmm," said Boris, "I don't think we have that in Morovia."

He thanked her and went out to find his parents. Their scones were getting cold.

His parents had been shopping. Randall was wearing a brand-new kilt with a sporran and a matching beret.

"Apparently it's McLupus tartan!" he said proudly. "Handsome, isn't it? I'm just trying to work out if the tail is worn under or over the kilt."

Boris was glad none of his friends in Morovia could see them. He wasn't sure wolves were supposed to wear kilts.

At least they hadn't bought a tartan carpet.

Leonora pointed to the real estate office.

"What do you think, Boris? Come and see!"

There, in the window, was a picture of Drommuir Castle. It was for sale!

"Are we going to buy it?" asked Boris. Could they do that? he wondered. Just buy a castle?

"Well," said Leonora, "we weren't planning to buy a castle. But if it's for sale then we can ask to look inside. That would be fun, don't you think?"

Boris was interested to see that Mr. Vorslad was chatting to a man inside the real estate office. Randall and Leonora noticed too. The wolves all had a closer look. They stared in, pressing their noses against the glass. At that moment, Mr. Vorslad turned toward the window.

He nearly leaped out of his skin.

"**Aaaaaaaargh**!" he said.

"Uh-oh," said Randall. "Time to move on, perhaps …"

Extract from *A Guide to Morovia*
by Brydie Phelan

Most modern Morovian wolves wear simple breeches or skirts, woolen in winter and cotton in summer. Riding boots and leather sandals were fashionable in the past, but modern wolves prefer to go barefoot. Traditional clothing includes an embroidered waistcoat with several internal pockets for storing snacks.

Wolves avoid wearing fur as it confuses humans, who like to know which fur belongs to the wolf and which fur belongs to the clothes. Tartan is rarely worn, except by wolves with Scottish heritage.

RIDING BOOTS WORN WITH WOOLEN BREECHES

TYPICAL WAISTCOAT WITH FOOD POCKETS

FUR BREECHES RARELY WORN DUE TO CONFUSION

CHAPTER 8

Protecting Castles

The wolves took a hasty stroll by the harbor. While his parents talked about money and savings, Boris found some beautiful, smooth pebbles in different shades of gray. He decided to collect them as souvenirs. Boris imagined his Scots pebble collection growing magnificently. He started the collection immediately, popping some of the smoothest, roundest stones in his backpack.

Half an hour later, they went back to the real estate office. Boris had to walk slowly and steadily. His backpack was lumpy and overflowing with pebbles.

"I hope Mr. Vorslad's gone," said Leonora. "We don't want to frighten him again."

If anyone deserved a scare it was nasty Mr. Vorslad, thought Boris, as they walked in. He was just about to tell them about Vorslad Villas when a tall man with slicked-back hair came to greet them.

The man looked them all up and down. Then he walked straight toward Randall.

"Good afternoon, sir. Are you interested in one of our properties?"

It was as if Boris and Leonora weren't even there! Boris glared. He put his hands on his hips and several pebbles tumbled from his backpack.

"Um, yes …" said Randall. "Drommuir Castle, we were wondering …"

"Oh no, I'm afraid not," interrupted the man. He sounded bored, as if he had better things to do with his time.

"There is significant interest in this property … and large sums of money involved," he added, flicking his wrist dismissively. "Not at all affordable, I'm afraid."

Boris wondered how the man knew what they could–or couldn't–afford. Anyway, they only wanted to look around.

"Ahem," said Leonora, smiling assertively.

Leonora's "assertive" smile was meant to be firm but fair. Of course, it was only used on rare occasions. On this particular occasion, Leonora's eyes glinted, three of her fangs popped out, and part of her gum was visible.

The man took a step back. Unfortunately some of Boris's pebbles had rolled onto the floor behind him. The man stumbled, lost his balance, and fell backward into a potted fern.

"Perhaps," said Leonora, "we could speak to the owner ourselves."

"It's not common practice …" said the man, trying to pull himself out of the plant pot. Dozens of tiny fern fronds were stuck to his shiny hair.

"We'll be very discreet," said Leonora, getting out an elegant leather notebook with gold edges. "Now kindly do pass on the details."

The wolves walked along Portlessie shore till they came to a white stone cottage set against a hill. Steps up the side led to a bright-red door, and on the door there was a brass lion's head with a door knocker in its mouth. Boris knocked once. And then he knocked a few more times because the lion knocker made a wonderful ringing sound when you knocked it, as well as a very loud knocking sound.

"Why, hello," said Aileen Fordyce, when she opened the door. "What a lovely surprise! And so much knocking! Come in!"

Boris liked Aileen's office at once. It was big and light. All round the edges were shelves crowded with books and huge wooden chests, their wonky drawers stuffed with drawings. Framed pictures of old buildings and maps covered the rest of the walls. At one end, a large bay window looked out to sea. Boris's pebble collection was heavy. He plonked himself on the window seat for a rest, and reached for a fluffy, striped cushion.

"Watch out for Tavish," said Aileen. "He doesn't like being woken up."

Two large green eyes appeared in the cushion. A dangly, stripy tail swished dangerously. Boris took his hand away.

"Don't show fear," said Aileen. "He'll come to you when he's ready."

Boris looked out at the choppy sea and the circling gulls. He tried not to think about Tavish's gleaming green eyes, or how sharp his claws might be.

"We're curious about Drommuir Castle," said Leonora. "Mr. McGrath, the real estate agent, said it's owned by Scots Conservation. But it's for sale ..."

"Drommuir, yes!" said Aileen. "We do own it. The problem is, it needs repairs."

"And that costs money, I suppose," said Randall, pulling up a chair. He put on his thinking glasses, which he used for looking intelligent in meetings.

"And the government used to give us money for repairs," said Aileen. "Drommuir Castle was protected, you see. We protect castles so we can look after them, and so they can't be knocked down."

The wolves gasped. Knocked down! A castle!

"But the government suddenly decided that Drommuir isn't 'historically significant.' That means it's not important enough to protect. Now that we don't get the money, we can't afford to fix Drommuir up and we've had to close it to the public just in case. It's such a shame." Aileen sighed.

"And someone wants to buy it?" said Leonora.

"Yes, and he's offering an awful lot of money."

Boris was looking at a "Say NO to Vorslad Villas" poster, just behind Aileen's desk. "It's Mr. Vorslad, isn't it?" he asked.

"Vorslad Villas!" said Leonora, looking at the

poster behind Aileen's desk. "Of course!"

"He wants to buy Drommuir and build his luxury resort there," said Aileen. "And he's a very rich man.

"Just look at this!" she said, handing Leonora one of Mr. Vorslad's brochures.

"Will he knock the castle down?" asked Boris, his heart sinking. Tavish was sitting on his lap now. The cat weighed more than his pebble-filled backpack.

"He plans to keep the bits with the turrets," said Aileen, "but he'll build all around it, and there's a sky tower."

"It's a disgrace!" tutted Leonora, as she leafed through the brochure.

"If Mr. Vorslad buys Drommuir, no one will be allowed there except rich guests who pay to stay," said Aileen. "Also, lots of birds nest in the dunes nearby, and there are deer, badgers, otters and owls in the forest.

"But Mr. Vorslad wants to cut down trees, drive out to the beach over the sand dunes, hunt in the forests and fish in the river."

"And blast salmon!" added Boris. He felt especially sorry for the salmon. And the puffins.

"Just appalling!" said Leonora, shaking her head. She sighed. "And Drommuir is so lovely. We walked there yesterday. There's something special about the place. I can't quite put my paw on it."

"The wealthy should act responsibly," added Randall. His expression was serious.

"Of course we don't want the Vorslad Villas deal to happen," said Aileen, "but we can't afford to keep Drommuir. And the government seems to be on Mr. Vorslad's side."

Even Tavish seemed upset about Vorslad Villas. He meowed irritably, and dug his claws into Boris's lap.

"Ow," said Boris.

"I'll tell you what," said Aileen, "let's go and have a look inside the castle now, while we still can. I'll give you a tour. It's a charming place."

"And Boris, are these your pebbles on the floor? I'll get a bag for them."

CHAPTER 9

Exploring Drommuir

Aileen's station wagon was parked on the shore. They drove past Portlessie's shops and harbor and up the "gentle but long" path to the castle. Boris's pebble collection chinked in the stout canvas bag Aileen had given him. Maybe, he thought, he should collect fewer pebbles each day–just a few extra smooth ones.

To Boris's joy, the gray dog bounded up to them, woofing happily.

"It's that wolfhound," said Aileen. "Let's tie her up. I'll take her home afterward and try to find her owner."

The dog licked Boris under the chin.

"Hello, hello," said Boris, rubbing her ears. He tied the dog to a tree with a rope from Aileen's car. "Calm down!" he told her. It was hard to tie knots while she was slobbering all over him.

Aileen opened the solid wood door to Drommuir. "Come on in!"

They stepped down into a small hallway, with a grand stone staircase to one side. Through an archway was an open chamber with more doors.

"Where do the doors lead?" asked Boris. He was desperate to explore.

"Go and look," said Aileen. "Just be careful on the balcony. And leave your pebbles behind."

Boris opened every door and climbed every staircase. His favorite staircase went up in a spiral with mysterious doors all the way up. Each door led to a different bedroom. Boris's favorite bedroom had yellow walls and turret towers and looked over the forest to the sea. His least favorite bedroom had cold, blue walls and a painting of a fierce lady over the fireplace. The lady's eyes seemed to follow Boris around the room.

Boris opened a door at the top of the stairs and found himself in a long room with a balcony. The view was magnificent. He could see across the bay, to the village and cliffs behind, the beach and the harbor and across to the Highland Hotel.

There was a bell in the middle of the balcony. The bell rope dangled just within reach.

I wonder if the bell rings, thought Boris.

He grabbed the rope with both paws and gave it a firm tug. The bell swung. Then it rang!

DONG!

Boris grinned.

Then, the bell swung the other way and suddenly the rope pulled back.

DONG!

Boris was flung along the stone floor. As he let go of the rope, he fell forward. He stumbled toward the edge, tripped and landed between two jutting battlements.

"Aaaah! Help! Help!" he shouted. Boris's hind legs were kicking in the air behind him, and his head and front legs were stuck on the outside, hanging over the edge.

The bell was still swinging. *Dong, dong, dong!*

Boris's head swam. The ornamental moat and the little bridge were below. Very, very far below. Now the view didn't seem so magnificent. Just terrifying. Boris reached behind with his front paws and tried to pull himself back onto solid ground, but he was trembling too much.

Then something started tugging at his feet.

Boris felt warm, wet breath on his back paws.

It was the gray dog.

Boris wriggled. The dog tugged at his hind legs. And at last, after much huffing and puffing, Boris fell back onto the balcony floor.

"Ow!" The stone was hard. Fortunately Boris had landed on the softer, hairy dog.

"You got free!" said Boris, rubbing his bruised leg. He was glad that his knots weren't that good. The dog barked and swished her tail. She didn't seem hurt at all. "Clever dog!"

On the way down, Boris saw he'd missed a small, arched door just off the stairwell. The door opened onto a secret-looking passage with rough walls. At the end was another little door. Boris opened this door carefully. He'd had enough surprises for one day.

He and the dog were on a balcony, which overlooked a cheerful hall full of comfy antique furniture.

Below them, Aileen, Randall and Leonora wandered the hall, surveying the many paintings and sculptures around the walls.

"Yoo-hoo!" Boris waved down at them.

"So who owned the castle before?" Leonora was asking.

"The McBride family," said Aileen. "Their ancestors stormed the castle and took it by force, hundreds of years ago. That's all we know. The McBrides sold the castle to Scots Conservation about fifty years ago. Most of the people in the paintings are McBrides."

The people in the paintings looked disapproving, as if the wolves had no business looking at them.

Like the fierce old woman in the blue room, Boris thought.

Randall was examining the paintings. As a polymath, he was also an expert in historical art.

"A marvelous Raeburn!" he said knowledgeably. "Whereas this pastoral scene is a fine example of eighteenth-century Romanticism."

"Mr. Vorslad wants all the paintings too," said Aileen.

Boris was intrigued by two carvings on either side of the little balcony. They looked like wolf heads, but more ferocious than any wolves he knew. He propped his notebook on the stone rail and did a quick drawing.

Randall was still being an expert about art, so Boris went back downstairs.

The ground floor chamber was long, with a huge fireplace at one end. The dog lay down in front of it, looking entirely at home.

Boris examined the fireplace. There was a little, flat carving in the middle. It was paw shaped, just like the one by the front door.

With a crash, the front door flew open.

"Of *course* we can go in," said a man's voice. "It'll be my castle soon enough!"

The man chuckled smugly, and Boris heard a woman laugh.

"That sounds like Mr. Vorslad," said Aileen, coming downstairs. "He's not supposed to be here! Oh, I can't be bothered with him today. Quick! Let's sneak out the back corridor. Come on, doggie!"

But the dog stood by the chamber door, her back arched. Suddenly she lurched toward the main entrance.

"Woof!" she barked. "Woof, woof, GRRRR!"

This seemed to surprise Mr. Vorslad. There was a kerfuffle and a splashing noise.

"My coffee! Get away, beast!" he yelled. "What is

this horrible animal doing here? I won't have dogs in my castle!

"Owww! It scalded me!"

"It's just coffee," said the woman's voice. "It'll come out."

"Ha! I'll catch the rascal," said a male voice. Boris thought the voice sounded like Mr. McGrath, the real estate agent.

But the dog streaked past Boris and out the back corridor. She flew toward Aileen's station wagon and into the passenger seat.

Hastily the Greycoats jumped into the back seat of Aileen's station wagon. As they whizzed out the gate, they passed Mr. Vorslad and his friends in the grounds. Mr. Vorslad had taken off his green tweed jacket. He was standing at the little stone bridge, while Mr. McGrath made notes on a clipboard.

It's not even his castle yet, thought Boris, glaring out the window. Mr. Vorslad scowled back. Boris was pleased to see the coffee had gotten onto his shirt, tie and trousers too. *He must have just emptied it all over himself. Imagine blaming the dog!*

"What did you think of Drommuir?" Aileen asked the wolves as they drove toward the Highland Hotel.

"It was perfect," sighed Leonora. "Wouldn't it be lovely to buy it?"

"I thought we were just looking," said Boris, surprised.

"We've been talking," said Randall. "There's something about Drommuir …"

"Mr. McGrath said we could never afford it," said Boris. He scowled. He didn't like the rude real estate agent.

"Mr. Vorslad is exceedingly rich," said Aileen. "And it seems he'll pay anything for this castle. I don't understand it. There are lots of other places he could build his horrible villas."

"If we wolves were to own Drommuir," said Randall, seriously, "we would be model custodians."

"That means we'd look after it properly," explained Leonora to Boris.

"I'd love to sell Drommuir to you," said Aileen. "But it's not up to me, sadly. I'll find out how much money Mr. Vorslad is offering. If you can offer more then you may be in with a chance."

Aileen dropped the wolves, and Boris's bag of pebbles, at their hotel.

"I'll get in touch as soon as I know," she said.

Boris waved to the dog as the car pulled away.

After supper, Boris had a lovely time arranging the pebbles on his dresser.

He organized them by size, and then by roundness, and then by size again. He arranged the pebbles in towers, which toppled down now and again. After a while, Leonora suggested that Boris might want to read about his Scottish ancestors in bed. Quietly.

So Boris got out *The History of the Scottish Greycoats*.

After the deaths of his brothers, Rufus, the second Baron McLupus and only surviving triplet, inherited Wolfemina Hall. Soon, he had five sons, quintuplets Fergus, Felan, Foyle, Fenris and Fridolf.

Of course, as soon as the young wolves were old enough to hold a sword, they started to fight over Wolfemina Hall. Poor Rufus and Morag just wanted

Rufus, his wife, Morag, and their adorable quintuplets

a peaceful life. They snuck away by night and traveled in disguise to Morovia, where they settled in the forest.

Back in Scotland, the five McLupus sons waged battle after battle to see who would get Wolfemina Hall. These bloody skirmishes lasted for many years, with hideous losses on all sides.

Rufus, his wife, Morag, and their deplorable quintuplets

Boris wondered why the brothers couldn't just share Wolfemina Hall. It would be boring living there alone, anyway.

He rearranged his pebbles one more time, in order of smoothness, and settled down to sleep.

CHAPTER 10

Kiltercalder Palace

The next morning, over breakfast in the hotel dining room, the wolves decided to take a day trip.

"It will distract us from thinking about Drommuir," said Leonora.

"Can we see another castle?" asked Boris.

Discreetly, he passed a morsel of black pudding under the table, where Hamish was camped out by his feet.

"A different kind of castle, though," he explained. "A big one, with dungeons and battlements!"

"And with a gallery of fine artworks," added Randall, nodding.

"I'd like to go to a castle where I can look at pottery and tartans," said Leonora. "Historic furniture, maybe … and beautiful old vases. That kind of thing."

Boris knew exactly that kind of thing.

Ugh, he thought, *I'll be bored stiff.*

There were dozens of tourist brochures in a stand nearby. Hastily, Boris flicked through *The Definitive Guide to Scottish Castles*. At last, he found somewhere to suit them all. Kiltercalder Palace had spooky, medieval dungeons and an underground tunnel, as well as a wax museum and a Royal Gallery. It also had a café and a gift shop.

There's bound to be a few old jugs and carvings in the Royal Gallery, thought Boris. *And I can climb the ruins and hide in the dungeon. And buy fudge in the gift shop!*

"How about this," he said. "There are old vases and stuff."

"Good work, Boris!" said Leonora. "That looks perfect."

"Indeed," said Randall. "Very historic!"

Soon they were outside the Highland Hotel, ready to go. Leonora wore a country shooting jacket and a long tartan skirt. Randall had on his new kilt and tartan beret.

Randall handed Boris a matching hat, with a woolly pompom on top.

"I bought this yesterday!" he said proudly. "Now we all match!"

Boris sighed and put it on.

The Bentley drove up to meet them. Boris was happy to see Jim at the wheel. He waved and indicated his new tartan hat. Jim smiled sympathetically.

"Kiltercalder," said Jim, opening the door for Boris, "good choice! We'll see some mountains on the way."

As they meandered through the mountains, the light changed.

The mountains changed too. They were misty and moody, then they were fierce and foreboding, then grand and golden.

Soon, they were stuck behind a slow trail of campers. The road was winding and narrow. Boris started to feel carsick.

"Roll your window down," said Jim. "And look out the front. Have a ginger ale too. Ginger's good for car sickness."

Well, that's useful, thought Boris, *because I love ginger ale.*

At last, they arrived at a sparkling lake.

"This is what's known as a 'loch,' in Scots," said Randall.

Kiltercalder Palace sat on top of a craggy mound, overlooking the loch. It was rugged and splendid, and had huge walls with knobbly battlements and big crumbling towers with arrow slits. Behind the towers, jagged ruins loomed against the open sky.

"It's dramatic all right," said Jim.

They parked by the lake and climbed the steps to the palace. The entrance was between two solid towers, across a wooden drawbridge.

It's like one of the paintings in my book, thought Boris. He imagined Scottish warriors thundering across the bridge on horseback and palace soldiers firing cannons, shooting arrows and pouring boiling oil from the battlements.

They entered a courtyard, dotted with ruins. Leonora paid the entrance fee, while Randall and Boris read about the palace. Kiltercalder was nearly 800 years old. It had been burned down and rebuilt twice. Then it had started to crumble, until an earl of somewhere decided to rescue it. Now the palace was protected.

Unlike Drommuir, thought Boris, sadly.

"Can I go to the wax museum, while you and Mum look at paintings and vases?" said Boris.

"I don't see why not," said Randall. "Waxworks make your mother feel sick, if I remember correctly."

The wolves booked a Spooky Dungeon Tour for later on.

"I'm slightly peckish after that drive," said Leonora.

"It wouldn't be good," said Randall, "to do a tour when we're peckish."

To avoid getting hungry, and any Undignified Situations that might arise, the wolves went straight to the Kilty Café. After making themselves comfortable by the cake counter, the Greycoats waited to be served.

The café was cozy and bustling, and the cakes looked magnificent.

"How many are we allowed to have?" Boris asked.

"I think we may as well try a few," said Leonora.

"I am terribly hungry," said Randall, licking his chops and looking around. An elderly lady, who had been watching them fearfully, let out a muffled scream.

Boris was glad Leonora hadn't noticed this. He didn't think it was a good time for one of her reassuring smiles.

The café sold nine different kinds of cake: coffee, vanilla, jam, strawberry, chocolate, lemon, caramel, fruitcake and carrot.

After some thought, the wolves chose strawberry cake, jam cake and lemon cake.

After more thought, the wolves decided to try all of the cakes, except the carrot cake, several times over. They were careful with the chocolate ones. Too much chocolate is not good for wolves. Also, being polite and respectable, they ensured there was some cake left over for other customers.

Boris hoped that the other visitors liked carrot cake more than they did.

After their snack, Randall and Leonora left for the Royal Gallery.

"I hope the people in the paintings aren't all McBrides this time," Leonora was saying.

I hope the waxworks aren't McBrides too! thought Boris, as he entered the wax museum by himself. It sounded scary enough already.

The first display was a violent battle scene, showing soldiers defending the palace against the Stewarts. There were waxworks of men slashing each other with swords, being pierced with arrows and covered in boiling oil. There was even a wax head on a stake.

Yuck! Boris could see why waxworks made his mum queasy. Quickly he walked on.

The next display was of famous Scots in heroic poses. There was "William Wallace," "Robert the Bruce" and even someone called "Alexander the Wolf." But Alexander didn't look at all like a real wolf, just a fierce human.

Boris hopped over the rope and into the display to get a closer look. Did Alexander have whiskers at least?

Just then, a couple of visitors came in.

Boris froze.

"I enjoyed that last display!" said a large man in a suit. "Wonderfully gory!"

"Look!" said a lady with a loud voice. "Someone called Alexander the Wolf, ha ha ha!"

Her laugh boomed around the room.

"Is this his pet wolf?" asked the man.

He pointed a stubby finger at Boris.

"It seems weird to put a hat on it!"

Boris had forgotten he was still wearing the tartan hat. And inside, too! "Manners!" Leonora would say.

Boris took his hat off.

"Huh?" said the man in the suit. "Hey! It moved! It must be some kind of robot wolf! Look!"

He turned to the lady, who was busy poking Robert the Bruce.

"How do they get his kilt on?" she was asking. "Ha ha ha!"

Boris slipped behind Alexander the Wolf's kilt and snuck to the back of the room. He crawled underneath a heavy black curtain and wriggled out the other side.

He found himself in a round stone room with narrow, arrow-slit windows. Posed by one of the windows was a waxwork of a heroic Scottish warrior with a big black beard.

Boris hauled himself up to the window and looked out. He could see the parking lot, and the loch, far below.

"Imagine shooting an arrow from here," he said aloud.

"You'd need a good aim," said the warrior, from behind his beard.

Boris nearly fell backward.

"You're alive?" he said, once his fur had flattened down again.

"I'm not made out of wax," said the warrior.
"If that's what you were thinking."

"Um … So who are you?" asked Boris.

"I'm Murdo McMurtrie," said the warrior, "and
I'm dressed for battle. Me and my group do battle
reenactments. We dress up and stage battles all over
the Highlands. We're doing one later today."

He was beaming. Boris could see that Murdo
McMurtrie loved to battle.

"With arrows and boiling oil?" asked Boris.

134

Murdo McMurtrie laughed. "Not exactly … we just wave our swords around these days. No heads on spikes!"

"Whose side are you battling on?" asked Boris.

"We change about," said Murdo. "Today I'm a Stewart, fighting the Duke of Argyll. But first I'm giving the next dungeon tour."

He checked his watch. "It's time! I'd better go."

"I'm coming too," said Boris.

Boris and Murdo walked back to the courtyard to meet the tour group. Randall was giving a free Scottish history lecture to the waiting group, all about the Stewarts and King Charles.

"I found a warrior," announced Boris, "who's going to show us the dungeon."

Murdo led them all into a tower, then through several large chambers and down spiral stairs to the dungeon. The dungeon was cold, dank and reeked of history. It was dimly lit and there were chains hanging from the walls. They all took turns to look into a gruesome pit where, hundreds of years ago, enemies were thrown to their doom.

Murdo told the group terrifying tales of dreadful deeds, and of the ghosts that roamed Kiltercalder's dungeons. The stories were enjoyable, even though they were nasty. But the group all left a little chilled. As they walked back through the castle chambers, the walls didn't look quite as friendly as they had going in.

The wolves lagged behind.

"I'm not sure I believe in ghosts, but I do believe in atmospheres," said Leonora.

"I must howl!" said Randall, suddenly.

"Must you, dear?" said Leonora. "Now?"

"I'm sorry, my darling, but when a wolf must, a wolf must …"

And Randall stepped into a nearby chamber, leaned back and opened his throat.

"ArooooOOOooooooo!
... ArooooooOOOO!
AroooOOOOOOOO!"

"Arooooo!" echoed off the walls. "Arooooooooo!"

"Aroooooo ... Arooooo!" echoed in the dungeons below.

"It really carries, doesn't it, Mum," said Boris, desperately wishing he was somewhere else.

"AroOOOooOOOooooo!"
echoed eerily from the loch below.

"AroOOOOOOooOO!"

"Well," said Randall, cheerfully, "I think I'm done."

They emerged into the courtyard, where there was some kind of commotion. A group of people were crowded around the large man in the suit, who was leaning against the wall, his face pale.

"I heard it!" he cried. "The howling ghost of Kiltercalder! It chills me to the bone!"

"Maybe it was Alexander the Wolf?" said his lady friend, looking puzzled.

"Hey!" she yelled, seeing Randall. "Are *you* Alexander the Wolf?"

"Certainly not!" said Randall. "If you read your history you'll learn that Alexander the Wolf was a terrible individual. Utterly barbarous."

"Nothing like a real wolf at all!" added Leonora.

The wolves stopped by the "I Scream" kiosk by the dungeon entrance. They bought a "shiver shake" each, as well as a dozen chocolate "cone chillers," and made their way back to the car.

"Thank you!" said Jim, as Boris handed him a chiller cone. "How was it? Were you scared in the dungeon?"

"It was very educational," said Boris. "And the dungeon wasn't frightening at all—not for us, anyway!"

At the Highland Hotel, Aileen had left a message for the wolves to call her. Leonora rang straightaway, while Randall and Boris hung around nearby, trying to hear the conversation on the other side.

"Hello, Aileen!" she said. "Yes, it's us!"

Then she said, "Oh, really …" and her ears drooped. "That much? Yes, I see your point.

"Well, there's nothing we can do about it. No. Thank you."

Leonora put down the phone and turned to Randall and Boris.

"My dears," she said, "I'm sorry to say that we can't buy Drommuir Castle. Mr. Vorslad is offering an utterly enormous amount of money—way more than we can possibly match."

"So Mr. McGrath was correct," Randall said sadly.

As they trudged back up to their room, Boris imagined Mr. Vorslad strutting around Drommuir's grounds, blasting salmon and knocking down everything in his way.

Who was going to protect Drommuir? Was it just all about money?

CHAPTER 11

Bad News on the Beach

It was a gray, drizzly sort of morning, and the wolves were relaxing in the Jacobite suite.

"Can we *not* do a big trip today?" said Boris. "I want to work on my pebble collection."

Since their day at Kiltercalder Palace, the wolves had taken fishing trips, explored beaches, waded in rivers and climbed windy peaks. They'd bought antiques, souvenirs, tartan, crockery and cake. The day before, they'd gone on a train ride over a dramatic bridge to the west coast and purchased several tins of fudge. Then they had taken the train back, polishing off the fudge on the way.

Only two weeks had passed, but already Morovia and the Trans-Bohemia Express seemed a long time ago.

Boris's pebble collection was spreading under his bed and across the room. At the moment, he was sorting the smallest, roundest pebbles into empty fudge tins. *Clink* went the pebbles as he dropped them into the tins. *Clink, clink, clink!*

"I think you should return some of those pebbles to the beach," said Leonora, frowning slightly. "And maybe get a different hobby."

Leonora's new hobby was studying Celtic knot work patterns that joined together in never-ending twists and swirls. She was planning to design her own range of Celtic tea towels.

Randall had started to learn the Scottish bagpipes, but the manager of the Highland Hotel had asked him to please stop learning them on the grounds.

Now Randall was learning Scottish hammer throwing. The hotel manager had asked him to please learn a long way from the Highland Hotel.

Boris studied his pebbles. He was running out of room. Maybe he could take some pebbles back. And get a few new, smoother ones.

"Okay," he said, "can we go to the beach today?"

"I would like to spot a rare speckled lapwing," said Randall, looking up from his paper, "but we're going to a distillery after lunch, to see whisky being made."

"Well, I'm only a cub and not at all interested in whisky," said Boris, firmly. "And it will be a tour with lots of waiting and questions about whisky. And no dungeons or puffins or hauntings or beaches or cake."

"Mmm," said Leonora, "well, we're still going."

"Maybe I could go to the beach by myself?" asked Boris. "I won't go in the water and I'll be back by four."

His parents looked at each other. Boris thought they seemed relieved.

"I don't see why not," said Randall, "as long as you remember to pack lunch."

"And take a snack," said Leonora.

As Boris set off, the drizzle turned to a light mist. *A drizzly mizzle*, Boris thought.

He ambled along the beach, pebbles chinking in the pockets of his raincoat.

Up on the hill, Drommuir's turrets poked out of the forest. Soon, there would be a shiny new tower overshadowing the castle and the beach, and no one would be allowed to visit except Mr. Vorslad and his wealthy guests.

Boris's heart sank. It was so unfair.

There were trucks on the beach, near the forest. People in yellow hats were taking measurements. A digger was moving rocks and dumping piles of sand and mud near the dunes. The castle wouldn't be sold until the end of the week, Aileen had said. But Mr. Vorslad was already clearing the way for his horrible villas.

How dare he! thought Boris.

There were people near the base of the steps, holding up signs. Boris recognized the fishmonger, and Murdo McMurtrie.

Murdo looked different without his battling

costume. He was wearing a leather blacksmith's apron over normal clothes. Boris was pleased to see that Murdo's bushy black beard was real.

He waved, and Murdo waved back.

Mrs. McKay, from the tea shop, was taking photos of the diggers.

"Hello, Boris dear!" she said. "Look! The cheek of it … They're churning up the sand already! I'm sending these photos to the paper."

Boris felt terrible for the people of Portlessie, and for their lovely beach and forest.

"It's awful," he said. "Don't birds live in the sand?"

"Of course–not that these folks care!" said Mrs. McKay. "If we could only find a speckled lapwing … That would make the beach a conservation site. No diggers then!"

She patted Boris on the shoulder.

"I don't believe those nasty signs, by the way. We know what's behind it all!"

"Me neither," said a woman nearby. "I'm Elsie. Pleased to meet you. I hope your father is enjoying his new kilt from my shop!"

"Um, thank you," said Boris. "He wears it every day. I hope you can stop the diggers. Good luck."

He wandered toward the shore. The tide was low and the tide pools would be full of fascinating–and tasty–sea animals. *What nasty signs?* Boris wondered as he trudged across the wet sand. Surely nothing to do with him?

Two little children with buckets and nets were peering into a tide pool. Boris recognized them from Mrs. McKay's tea shop. He wondered what they'd found.

"Is it a sea anemone?" he asked.

Boris loved sea anemones. It was fun to watch them turn from a jelly blob into an underwater flower and then back into a blob.

"An enemy?" said the girl, her eyes widening. "Are you an enemy?"

The children's mum was nearby. She turned round, saw Boris, and gasped. She scooped up the little girl and led the boy away by the hand.

"It's fine, dear," Boris heard her say. "There's nothing to be frightened of."

Boris stared after them. His tail drooped.

Frightened of him? He was only a cub!

He looked down at his face, reflected in the water. He didn't look scary at all. Just sad.

And there were no sea anemones, only mussels and seaweed.

Boris gathered some mussels and trudged back along the beach, snacking on the mussels as he went.

The protesters had left, but the diggers were still

working away. There was a big car too. Some men in business suits and heavy jackets got out.

Boris pulled the hood of his raincoat down over his snout and walked past quickly.

"And of course that section of forest will have to go," a man was saying. Boris recognized his voice from the day at Kiltercalder Palace. "Anyway, Scotland has plenty of otters and stuff already."

"Ha ha ha!" said a lady, loudly. "And loads of forest. We can spare a few trees!"

Under his hood, Boris scowled.

"Hey, look!" said the man, pointing out to sea. "Do ya think those black things are seals?"

"They're rocks," said Boris, loudly, from behind a grassy mound. "Grrrrr ..."

And he stomped off, leaving them staring after him open-mouthed.

Once Boris was a safe distance from the diggers, he flopped on the sand by a dune.

What a miserable day!

Then he looked up. And straightaway Boris knew what Mrs. McKay meant by "nasty signs."

By the dune was a huge sign. It wasn't a friendly sign. It said:

WOLVES: A SIGNIFICANT THREAT

Concerned about the arrival of wolves in Portlessie? You should be! Wolves are savage animals and can destroy our countryside!

There was a crest on the sign. Below it were the words "Clan McBride."

Boris stared at the sign, his mind whirling. "Significant threat!"

Could this mean him? And his mum and dad? It must.

They were the only wolves in Portlessie. Why would anyone say they were savage? And what was Clan McBride? He'd heard the name before, but where?

Boris felt as if he had a huge, heavy rock in his tummy.

Suddenly a little crested bird appeared from behind a tuft. It dashed forward and nabbed one of Boris's mussels.

Boris couldn't believe it! Even the birds were against him.

As the bird nibbled on his mussel, Boris got out his sketchbook. Drawing always made him feel better.

He sketched the cheeky bird. It was a wonky sketch, because the bird kept hopping about. So Boris made notes next to the drawing. He didn't know a lot about birds, but he tried his best.

"Feet are orange, webbed and … small," he wrote. "Little crest on head, purple and green shiny bits, lots of dots on back."

After the drawing, Boris felt a bit happier.

He looked up at the sign. And sighed. Reading the words made Boris feel sad and small and worried, but he copied them into his notebook all the same.

Boris gave the bird the rest of his mussels and wandered back to the Highland Hotel.

He would have to tell his parents about that sign.

Back in the Jacobite suite, Randall was lying on the sofa. He was propped up with cushions and pillows and clutching a cloth to his forehead.

"We visited the distillery," said Leonora, passing Randall a steaming cup of tea. "Unfortunately your father was overcome by the fumes from the vats. He nearly fell in!"

"Perhaps I inhaled a little strongly," explained Randall, in a weak voice. "I recall feeling a tad wobbly around the knees and after that … Nothing …"

Boris stared at his father. How could anyone think they were savage or threatening? It was ridiculous! His father, a full-grown wolf, had just collapsed at a whiff of whisky.

"Poor love," said Leonora, popping a tartan blanket over Randall's hind legs. "What a day!"

Boris decided not to mention the sign for now. It didn't seem like the right time.

He went straight to bed after supper.

To distract himself, Boris got out *The History of the Scottish Greycoats*. The chapter opened on a painting of a dramatic battle scene. There were wolves and humans on all sides, fighting fiercely on a Scottish hillside. The wolves in the picture looked savage and threatening. So did the humans, of course. Trees had been chopped and the countryside was burning.

Boris shut the book. He couldn't bear to read on.

"Are people in Scotland afraid of us?" he asked Leonora, as she came to kiss him goodnight.

"Well," she said, "maybe now and again, but I think the important thing is to smile reassuringly. That always soothes their apprehensions.

"Sleep well, Boris, my love."

With his head on the red-and-gold tartan pillow, Boris gazed out the window at the gray sea below. It was still light, as they were so far north.

Are we a threat? he thought. *Maybe we shouldn't be here at all.*

And what's Clan McBride? Who made the sign? And why?

Thoughts swam through Boris's head and it took a long time for him to fall asleep.

The Battle of the Five Brothers

Boris didn't wake up till after ten.

Leonora brought him a cup of tea in bed.

"You had a lovely, long sleep," she said, "and so did your father, who is recovered from his whisky wipeout …"

Boris sat up. Then he remembered the day before.

The heavy feeling in his tummy came back. He had to tell his mum about the diggers. And the tide pools. And, most of all, the nasty sign about wolves. Wolves like them.

"Oh, dear," said Leonora, when Boris had finished his unhappy tale. "How awful. And the signs are

completely inaccurate, of course."

She hugged Boris. "Were you worrying about this last night?"

Boris nodded. He realized he was tearful thinking about it all, especially the family who hadn't wanted to talk to him.

Boris could tell that Leonora was upset too. But already she was making plans.

"You look pale round the muzzle," she said. "And Randall has had a shock. I think a bracing walk will be good for us all. I will ask the concierge to pack us a picnic."

Like most adult wolves, Leonora was fond of hearty walks and picnics.

"There's a Pictish standing stone I'd like to see too," she said. "Just up the hill from here. It's covered in wonderful knot work, apparently."

WOLF SNACKING BETWEEN MEALS

Extract from *A Guide to Morovia*
by Brydie Phelan

Most modern wolves need regular walks. Otherwise, even the most sophisticated wolf may become restless and start to damage furniture or eat between meals.

A successful wolf walk requires adequate supplies and refreshments:

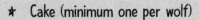

- ★ Cake (minimum one per wolf)
- ★ Sandwiches (carrot free)
- ★ Hot and cold drinks
- ★ Hats
- ★ Sunscreen for noses and tips of ears
- ★ Waterproofs (to prevent that embarrassing wet-wolf smell).

A well-planned wolf walk will also involve:

- ★ Foraging for food
- ★ Returning to a favorite spot and using finely honed investigative skills to detect who else has visited
- ★ A hunt of some sort, usually for monuments or buildings of interest
- ★ Regular picnic stops.

<u>NOTE:</u> Wolves have a low center of gravity and so get wet bellies easily. Walks in long grass are best avoided.

After a light breakfast of bacon, eggs, kippers, sausages, toast and more eggs, the wolves set out into the mist.

"We need to follow the little coast road for a mile or so," said Leonora, "away from Portlessie. Then we go across some fields and up a hill."

An hour later, the wolves were still trudging along the coast. The air was damp and misty and Randall's map was getting soggy.

"According to this map, there's an ancient battleground here somewhere," he said, peering into the mist.

Finally the wolves reached a hand-carved sign. It said "Stone of Crannoch," with an arrow pointing toward what might be a hill. It was hard to see in the mist.

The wolves had a brisk picnic to keep them going. Then they walked in the direction of the arrow.

"The stone should be here somewhere," said Leonora, after they'd crossed several fields.

Randall was at the front. "I think we've taken a wrong turn. I can't see any sign of a stone."

"Look!" cried Boris.

Behind Randall, a jagged shape loomed out of the mist.

It was the Stone of Crannoch.

Boris ran toward the stone. It was carved with twisting, curving patterns that wound around one another. Knot work!

One of the shapes looked just like a wolf's head. Boris found his notebook and thick black pencil and quickly took a rubbing. He didn't want his notebook to get damp.

Just then he heard a car door slam.

Through the mist, Boris could hear a voice–Mr. Vorslad's voice.

Not again! For a while that morning, Boris had forgotten about the nasty sign.

Now he felt sick.

He could see the silhouette of a huge black car. There must be a parking lot. Boris hid behind a stump.

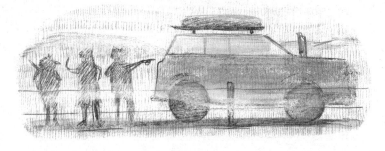

"Worth millions once it's properly developed," said Mr. Vorslad. "And the villagers will have to deal with it."

"They can't do a thing!" said another man, sounding smug.

"Shame about the fog," said Mr. Vorslad. "I wanted to give you an idea of the view. And show you where we'll be hunting."

Boris trembled with rage. He wished he could leap at Mr. Vorslad, waving a gigantic spike.

Fortunately he didn't have to.

A burly shape lurched out of the mist, sword in hand.

"Hurgggghggh!" it said.

"Arrrrgh!" said the man.

"HELP!" yelled Mr. Vorslad.

They rushed back to their car, slammed the door and drove off.

"Oops," said the figure. "Thought it was my mates. Didn't reckon there'd be visitors on a day like this."

It was Murdo McMurtrie, the bearded battle reenactor.

Randall and Leonora wandered into view.

"What a commotion!" said Leonora. "Is this your friend from the dungeon tour, Boris?"

Once they'd introduced each other, Murdo told the wolves about the day's plan. He and his friends were going to reenact the Battle of the Five Brothers.

"It actually took place between five rivals," said Murdo. "Very messy."

"And behold the miracle!" he added, gesturing at the parting clouds. "The sun may actually shine! Stay and watch. It'll be a blast!"

"We'd love to," said Randall.

"Yes, please!" said Boris and Leonora in unison.

As gentle sunshine emerged through the mist, the parking lot was starting to fill up with "Scottish warriors." There was a buzz of anticipation as they got their armor in place and shared battle plans.

The wolves set up their second picnic by the ancient stone and prepared to enjoy the battle.

The battle was spectacular, even though it was confusing.

But then battles probably are *confusing*, thought Boris.

Lots of people were hurling themselves at one another, waving swords and shouting. There were fake explosions as warriors fired muskets. Boris tried to work out which of the five clans was winning.

The last of the mist disappeared and, all at once, the scene looked strangely familiar.

Boris blinked. Where had he seen this before?

Of course!

In the distance, across the valley, the turrets and chimneys of Drommuir poked up from the forest.

And suddenly Boris had an idea. It was almost too marvelous to believe. He fumbled for his sketchbook and jotted down a few notes. *The History of the Scottish Greycoats* was back in the hotel room. Boris couldn't wait to get back to read it.

It was as if he'd been looking at the different pieces of a puzzle. And now, everything fit together.

Could it really be?

During the walk home, Boris's mind was whirling. He ran ahead, rushed up to his hotel room and opened *The History of the Scottish Greycoats*.

He was looking for the horrible battle scene from the night before.

And there it was. There were swords, clubs and muskets, smoke and hacked trees. To the right, there was a monumental stone. It was the Stone of Crannoch.

This was the Battle of the Five Brothers!

Just like the one today! thought Boris. *Except there were wolves fighting too!*

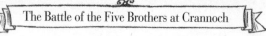

The Battle of the Five Brothers at Crannoch

It was almost unbelievable. Everything in his book had happened right where they were, near the Highland Hotel–and Drommuir Castle.

There was something else he needed to check. Trembling with excitement, Boris turned to an earlier chapter. Please let him be right!

There it was: "Lambert McLupus, in front of Wolfemina Hall."

Wolfemina Hall was painted small in the background, and slightly hidden behind Lambert's hat. But it looked very much like Drommuir Castle.

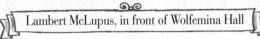
Lambert McLupus, in front of Wolfemina Hall

Boris grabbed his backpack and stuffed *The History of the Scottish Greycoats* inside, along with his sketchbook.

There was no time to lose.

"Mum! Dad!" he yelled. "I'm just popping down to the village!"

Significant Wolves

Boris walked along Portlessie's shore to a white stone cottage, and up the steps to a bright-red door.

Knock, knock, knock went the lion's head.

"Woof!" came from inside. "Woof, woof, woof!"

"Boris," said Aileen Fordyce, "come in! I'm having tea and muffins."

The big gray dog was delighted to see Boris. Once she had stopped licking him, Boris got comfy in a squishy chair. Tavish wasn't on his window seat. Boris looked around. A stripy tail hung dolefully from a drawer in Aileen's filing cabinet.

"He's sulking," said Aileen, "because of the dog.

And I can't find an owner for her. What to do?"

She sighed heavily. "Oh, Boris, it's just terrible. Drommuir is to be sold tomorrow! Mr. Vorslad is moving his diggers in."

"Can I show you something?" said Boris. "Something significant?"

Aileen looked surprised.

"Significant?" she said. "That sounds most mysterious, Boris! What have you brought to show me?"

Boris pulled *The History of the Scottish Greycoats* from his bag and opened it to the painting of Lambert McLupus in front of Wolfemina Hall.

"This is Wolfemina Hall, where our ancestors, the McLupuses, lived long ago."

Aileen stared.

Boris grinned. "Recognize it?" he said.

"Oh!" said Aileen. "It can't be!"

She grabbed her glasses. "There are a lot of castles that look like this, Boris," she said, inspecting the book, "but it does look very …"

Boris turned to "The Battle of the Five Brothers." "These are my ancestors too!" he said. "They're not behaving very well," he added, apologetically.

"The stone!" said Aileen. "I know that stone!"

"And look at what's behind it, in the trees." Boris pointed at the turrets and battlements. "I think that's Drommuir Castle, right here."

Together, they read the text below the painting.

After the horrifying battle of Crannoch, in which all five brothers and their followers fought for Wolfemina Hall, only one of the McLupus quintuplets remained. Fergus McLupus, the last brother, was fed up with fighting. He joined the clergy and set up an orphanage in Wolfemina Hall.

But the local McBride clan wanted Wolfemina Hall for themselves. They surrounded the castle, chased away the orphans and took over. Fergus McLupus was forced to leave his homeland or suffer the sword.

Aileen's eyes were shining.

"So the McBride clan took Wolfemina Hall by force from Baron Fergus McLupus," she said. "And Drommuir Castle once belonged to the McBrides!"

She dashed to a shelf and wrested down an enormous book. Boris read the title: *The Definitive and Correct Guide to Celtic Skirmishes*.

"This is very reliable," said Aileen, plonking the book on the table with a thump.

She leafed through the index.

"Here we go!" And she pointed at a passage of tiny writing. "It says Drommuir was taken over by the McBrides in 1670 CE. That sounds right!

"Oh, Boris," she said, "I think Drommuir Castle was actually Wolfemina Hall! But that doesn't mean it's yours—you do know that."

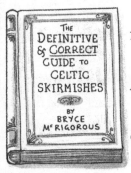

"I know," said Boris, "but it does mean that Drommuir is … "

"Historically significant!" said Aileen.

"And if it's significant, you can't change it!" said Boris. "Nobody can."

They stared at one another.

"I'm going to make a lot of calls now," said Aileen. Boris could see she was trying to stay calm. "And some of the calls might be difficult. You'd better pop home for now, Boris. I'll be in touch soon."

Boris was excited too. Things were about to improve, he just knew it.

"Good luck with the calls!" he said. "Um … can I have another muffin?"

"Here's a couple of muffins for the road," said Aileen, smiling.

She gave him a hug. "Thank you, Boris, you are a wonderful detective and a thorough historian! Can I hang on to your book for now? I'll be careful with it. See you later!"

Outside, a bright shaft of sunlight lit the sea.

Changes were afoot. Good ones. Boris was sure of it.

He wandered back along the beach. It was low tide again and gulls circled the tide pools, looking for food. The sea frothed across the sand, bringing lots of exciting new pebbles with it.

Boris nibbled his muffin and stared out to sea. He noticed a sudden movement behind a tuft of grass. It was the speckled little bird that stole his mussel. It hopped toward him, tilted its head to one side and stared meaningly at his muffin.

"Cakes are bad for birds," said Boris.

Down by the shoreline, the family from yesterday was making a sandcastle. He remembered they were frightened of him. Feeling sad, he started to move on.

Then he noticed that they were all waving to him. Boris waved back.

The little girl ran toward him. "We're building a castle! Want to join in?"

"Are you sure?" asked Boris.

Their mother came over.

"Hello there," she said. "I'm so sorry about yesterday. We're not used to wolves, I'm afraid. I saw that sign and got scared. I was being silly. We didn't mean to hurt your feelings." She smiled at Boris and put out her hand. "Please accept my apologies."

Boris put his paw in her hand and smiled back.

"I'm Irene," she said, "and this is Ellie and Jack. Can you help us with our moat?"

"I'm Boris–and yes, please!" said Boris. Moats were the best part of sandcastle making.

"We're digging a tunnel, I think," said Ellie.

"Great," said Boris, and he came over.

After a happy couple of hours digging, building and moat making, Boris said goodbye to Irene, Ellie and Jack and wandered back to the Highland Hotel.

Aileen's station wagon was already there. The dog was in the back, looking out mournfully. Boris stuck his paw through the window and petted her.

"I'm sure you'll get a walk soon," he said.

Boris found Aileen and his parents in the hotel dining room, surrounded by books and papers.

The History of the Scottish Greycoats by Baron McLupus the Fifteenth sat in the middle of a long table.

"Boris!" said Randall. "We're impressed!"

"We're so very proud of you," said Leonora.

And they both hugged him.

"Me too!" said Aileen. "Everyone agrees–Drommuir really is Wolfemina Hall. You've saved the castle!"

"It's an important part of Scottish history," said Randall, "so it needs to be protected."

"I had a feeling about that castle!" said Leonora.

"We should get some money to fix up Drommuir now," said Aileen, "and no one will be allowed to build there, or on the grounds. Not even Mr. Vorslad."

"So what will he do?" asked Boris.

"Mr. Vorslad has pulled out of the deal." Aileen smiled broadly. "I can't say he was happy about it. There will be no Vorslad Villas at Drommuir."

"Hooray!" said Randall.

"Yip, yip, yip," said Hamish, running into the room with a sock in his mouth. Boris hoped the sock belonged to Mr. Vorslad. Leonora gave Hamish one of her reassuring smiles. The little dog whimpered and dived under a chair.

"There's something else you should know," said Aileen. "It's probably not a surprise, but Mr. Vorslad made several libelous signs about wolves.

"He denied it, but it's obvious. He even put his family crest at the bottom."

"His family crest?" asked Boris.

Aileen pulled a document from her file. "I got this from the real estate office."

The document was called "Proposed Purchase of Drommuir Castle." The front page was signed–by "Mr. Thaddeus Rex McBride Vorslad."

"He's a McBride!" said Boris. "So it was his family castle too! His ancestors took it from Fergus McLupus."

"And then they sold it to Scots Conservation," Aileen reminded him. "So he has no claim to it."

"I thought all those portraits reminded me of someone," said Leonora.

Boris suddenly realized.

"Maybe he knew we were related to the McLupus family? And I signed something too. The petition in Mrs. McKay's tea shop. I signed it Boris Fenrir Wolfgang McLupus Greycoat."

Aileen was keen to go to Drommuir Castle right away, so Boris could point out all the wolf carvings.

"There are even wolf carvings on the Stone of Crannoch," said Boris. "I did a rubbing today, in my sketchbook."

"Well," said Aileen, "wolves have been part of Scottish history for a long time. You *are* very significant. May I have a look at your sketches later?"

"Of course," said Boris.

Aileen's station wagon was full of books, paperwork and the big, gray dog. So they traveled in convoy, with Jim the chauffeur driving the wolves.

"I always liked that castle," he said.

At Drommuir, the dog bounded out of the station wagon and galloped round the grounds.

"I wish she could live here," said Aileen. "I'm not supposed to have dogs at the office. And Tavish is miserable. He's sulking under the plan chest now and I can't get him out."

"It's a fine place," said their chauffeur, Jim, "though you need to fix that roof."

"A family estate," said Randall, "in Scotland." There was a dreamy expression on his face.

Leonora was studying the roof. "So how much do you think …"

Suddenly a huge black car roared up the driveway and screeched to a halt, nearly crashing into the Bentley.

"Oi!" yelled Jim.

Mr. Vorslad leaped out of the car.

"How *dare* you!" he shouted at them all, his face red as a beet. "You have no proof! Show me the documents!"

He strode toward Aileen, waving several photocopied sheets of paper. Mr. Vorslad was furious and disheveled. His ankles were scratched and his trouser legs shredded and torn. And the seat of his trousers had been ripped away, revealing a pair of purple boxer shorts with little gold stars.

Boris giggled, though he was scared of Mr. Vorslad.

"What is that beastly cub laughing at?" yelled Mr. Vorslad, pointing angrily at Boris.

"Mr. Vorslad!" said Aileen, outraged. "Those papers! Did you break into my office?"

"There was no one to let me in," he retorted. "And the place is a disgrace … Vicious animals pretending to be cushions!"

Tavish must have claimed his window seat once the dog had gone out, Boris realized.

"You had no business being there," said Aileen. "And Tavish doesn't like to be sat on. Nor do people, actually."

Mr. Vorslad was quivering. "It's a conspiracy! Lies!"

"If you mean the evidence that Drommuir Castle is historically significant, then it's all around you," said Aileen. "You may not like it, Mr. Vorslad, but wolves are a proud part of our history."

"Hear, hear!" said Jim.

"And the paperwork has been copied and sent out. You can't pretend Drommuir isn't significant now."

"Drommuir is a McBride castle!" shouted Mr. Vorslad. "My Scottish Estate!"

He was purple with rage. Even Aileen was looking nervous.

"Ahem," said Leonora. And she smiled.

Mr. Vorslad got the full benefit of Leonora's "forceful smile." Five teeth were showing, and her eyes glinted.

He stepped backward, and seemed to shrink a little. Boris almost felt sorry for him. Almost.

"You were going to knock much of Drommuir down and stick a revolving tower on top," said Leonora, "which is no way to treat a castle. And, yes, Drommuir did once belong to the McBrides. But they took it by force. And then they sold it, for money."

"To Scots Conservation," added Randall, "who are still the owners."

"And it's significant!" said Boris.

"So leave it alone," said Jim.

"Woof!" added the dog.

Now Mr. Vorslad had nothing to say. He stood there, quivering. Then he stomped off to his car, giving them a good view of his gold-starred undies. As the car roared away, Boris noticed a strip of Mr. Vorslad's underpants was trapped in the front door. The gold stars waved in the wind.

"Tavish," said Aileen, "is an excellent judge of character."

"Grrrr," said the dog.

Aileen looked round at them all.

"Now," she said, "as the owners of Drommuir Castle, we can sell to anyone we like, as long as they let us advise on its keeping."

The wolves were looking very bright eyed.

"Could we still buy it?" asked Randall, his tail wagging hopefully.

"I'll find out!" said Aileen.

There was one more thing, Aileen said. It was about Boris's sketchbook.

"What was that bird you drew, Boris?" she said.

"Oh, it's just a bird from the beach yesterday," said Boris.

"Let me see," said Randall. "Ooh!"

He pulled *The Guide to the Birds of Scotland* from his inside jacket pocket.

"Did it look a bit like this?" asked Randall, pointing at a page with a photo of the cheeky bird from the beach.

"Yes!" said Boris. "It looked exactly like that. It was next to Mr. Vorslad's sign."

"Wonderful," said Leonora. "Not the sign—I mean, the bird!"

"Well then, that is a rare speckled lapwing!" said Aileen. "And if it's nesting on our beach, then no one can try to dig it up again. I'll get our nature team down there right away."

That night, in the Jacobite suite, Boris read the next chapter of *The History of the Scottish Greycoats* to Randall and Leonora.

After the McBrides forced Fergus McLupus to leave Wolfemina Hall, he traveled south to Europe. Fergus, the third Baron McLupus, settled in Morovia with his parents, Rufus and Morag.

Boris was glad the family had gotten together again, but he felt sad about all the McLupuses who had died fighting one other.

"Wolves were welcome in Morovia," read Boris, "but the family changed their last name to Greycoat, after Fergus's grandmother Wolfemina Greycoat, just to be on the safe side."

"So that's why we're the Greycoats," said Leonora.

"So who made this book?" Boris asked. "Who was Baron McLupus the Fifteenth?"

"Hmm," said Randall, counting on his paws, "that would be your great-great-grandfather, Boris. He was a Greycoat, of course, but he wanted to keep his McLupus title. He was very proud of it.

"If I wished," he added grandly, "I could call myself Baron McLupus the Eighteenth!"

"And one day," added Leonora to Boris, "you could call yourself Baron McLupus the Nineteenth."

Boris didn't think he would. "Boris Fenrir Wolfgang McLupus Greycoat" was long enough already.

Rufus, Morag and Fergus McLupus

CHAPTER 14

Open Day at Drommuir

It was a month later, and everyone was preparing for open day at Drommuir Castle. After three weeks of rain, the sun had come out for the morning.

Boris sat on a comfy window seat in his new room with the yellow turrets. He was checking the cake orders for the day.

The shaggy gray dog snored gently in a patch of sunlight by Boris's feet. Aileen had put notices around Portlessie and the towns nearby, but no one had come to claim the dog. She seemed to think the castle was her home. In the end, everyone thought she should probably live there. Boris had decided to call her Nessie.

Although the sun was out, it was still cold. Boris remembered they had planned to spend all summer in Scotland. How long, he wondered, was a Scottish summer? Summer in Morovia was long and balmy.

He went down the winding stone steps to the main hall. Life had been busy at the castle. The moat had been cleaned out and filled with water, the balcony made safe and the roof fixed up.

And family heirlooms were arriving from Morovia. Their distinguished friend, the wolf Sir Luther Fangdolph, had come for a long stay. He was advising Aileen on wolf heritage. Meanwhile, Randall was setting up a library in the downstairs gallery. The paintings were changing too. The disapproving-looking McBride family portraits had been sent to the Scottish Portrait Gallery. Instead of McBrides, the wolves hung portraits of their many Greycoat and McLupus ancestors.

"Doesn't Rufus McLupus look splendid!" said Leonora. She spoke through the side of her mouth, which was set in a reassuring smile. This was because

she was getting her portrait done. It would sit above the fireplace, along with portraits of Randall and Boris.

"Very splendid," said Boris, looking up at the wall. "I've checked and I think we'll need more cakes. Can I call Mrs. McKay?"

Soon it was time for the official opening.

Boris was nervous. He hoped enough people would come. Would they like the castle? Had he ordered enough cake?

"It depends who's eating," Mrs. McKay had told him. "I've catered for four wolves, and up to a hundred people. As long as there's no more wolves, we should be fine."

The first person to arrive was Aileen. Then Murdo McMurtrie. He was out of his blacksmith's apron and dressed for battle again.

Jim turned up, with a bright-red broom.

"It's a traditional housewarming gift," he said. "The broom doesn't have to be red; I just like red."

Next came Boris's friends Jack and Ellie, and their mother, Irene.

"Will there be cake?" asked Ellie.

"Of course!" said Boris. "Come in! Do you want to see what's behind this little round door?"

He showed Jack and Ellie up to the balcony overlooking the hall. Below them, guests were arriving thick and fast. Soon the hall was bustling–full of people from the village admiring paintings and eating cake. Boris recognized the fishmonger, Jim the chauffeur, Elsie and the nice lady from the kilt shop. Mr. McGrath, the real estate agent, was there too. Boris noticed he was being extra polite to Leonora.

Boris, Jack and Ellie went down and made themselves useful, passing around jam scones and bannocks.

Soon, it was time for speeches. Sir Luther Fangdolph rang a bell and called for quiet.

"Welcome to this wonderful castle!" said Aileen Fordyce. "As you may know, our hosts the Greycoats have a long Scottish heritage. Over three hundred years ago, their ancestors were forced to flee our land. But now, we are happy to welcome wolves once more."

"Hooray!" called Murdo McMurtrie. "Welcome home!"

"Thank you," said Leonora, graciously.

"And these marvelous wolves deserve the warmest welcome," added Aileen. "If it wasn't for them, we wouldn't be standing here today. But now … there will be no Vorslad Villas!"

Everyone cheered. Even Mr. McGrath clapped, though rather nervously as Leonora was smiling at him through the crowd.

"And finally, an extra cheer for Boris here." Aileen pulled a shy Boris to the front of the crowd.

"Boris has discovered a rare speckled lapwing on the dunes," she said. "And so our lovely beach will become a nature reserve. This is good news for our native birds, and for the beach!"

"Three cheers for Boris! Three cheers for the wolves!"

Next, it was Sir Luther's turn.

"Now, everyone," he said, "we will be stepping outside into the sunshine, for the unveiling of our new castle gates!"

Everyone followed Nessie as she bounded down the driveway.

The older, rusty gates had been removed, and there was a big sheet draped between the gateposts.

"It's time for the big reveal!" said Sir Luther, grandly. "Drommuir Castle is now to be known as …"

He whisked the sheet away.

"Wolfemina Hall!"

"Hooray!" cheered the crowd.

"Woof, woof," said Nessie.

"Honk," said a nearby peacock.

The new gates, welded by Murdo McMurtrie, were splendid. Among the twisting Celtic shapes and wolf emblems, Boris read the words "Wolfemina Hall–all welcome!"

Murdo beamed. His battle outfit suited him perfectly, from his tartan shawl, right down to his thick leather boots. Boris noticed Randall studying Murdo with interest. He hoped his father wasn't going to start dressing like a historic warrior.

Next, it was Leonora's turn to speak.

"Thank you, everyone," she said. "And now we have an announcement."

Boris sighed. He knew what was coming next.

"Much as we love it in Scotland," continued Leonora, "we have business to attend to at home. We will be leaving in a few days for our home in Morovia, though we will be back here regularly."

"We're going to come back in the summers," Boris explained to Jack and Ellie. "And I'll send you postcards from Morovia."

"The castle and its grounds will be open to the public six days a week!" added Leonora. "Sir Luther and Aileen Fordyce are in charge. There is to be a tea shop, supplied by Mrs. McKay from Tea by the Sea, whose wonderful scones and cakes we all know so well."

There were cheers of approval.

"And now, there will be some performances. Thank you, everyone!"

Randall was the first to perform.

As a polymath, he had been writing poetry in Scots. However, Aileen had persuaded Randall against reading his poetry aloud.

"Not everyone will be able to follow it," she had said.

Instead, Randall howled a Morovian folk tune while performing a Scottish sword dance. It was a bold performance, though it went on for some time.

"AaarooooOOOooooooOOOoooooo!!"

After an emotional final verse, Randall took a bow. The crowd clapped.

"Thank you," said Randall, "I'm glad you enjoyed my introduction. Now for the main performance!"

Once Randall had completed the first act of his performance, involving the bagpipes and a daring Highland Fling, Leonora stepped in.

"It is time," she said firmly, "for Boris to share his research!"

Boris was nervous at first, but soon he was enjoying sharing the dramatic tales from *The History of the Scottish Greycoats*.

Everyone gasped when Boris told of Lyall and Lowell McLupus falling in the moat in their armor. They were horrified at the plot to poison Remus McLupus. And there were tears when Boris revealed how the McBrides had forced Fergus McLupus and the orphans from Wolfemina Hall.

"You can read more about our ancestors and the battles, betrayals and hauntings at Wolfemina Hall here!" said Boris, holding up his book for everyone to see.

Finally it was Murdo McMurtrie's turn. He, and several dozen friends from the Scottish Battle Society, performed The Eleventh Battle of McLupus. This had taken place between three of the McLupus quintuplets.

Everyone settled onto the front lawn to watch the battle. It was highly dramatic. There were battlers on the outside balcony. One of the warriors even staged a dramatic fall from the bridge into the new moat. This terrified a nearby peacock. It ran across the lawn into a rhododendron bush, scattering several tail feathers.

"What a wonderful afternoon," said Aileen, handing a feather each to Jack and Ellie. "A total success." She looked sad. "Portlessie won't be the same without you all, Boris."

CHAPTER 15

In Safe Hands

A fortnight later, rain had set in and the Scottish summer appeared to be over for good.

The wolves were due to leave that afternoon. The little yellow room with the turrets would become a guest room for the winter. Boris was looking forward to seeing Greycoat Hall again, but he would miss Scotland and his new friends, especially Nessie.

"She can guard Wolfemina Hall," said Leonora. "It really is her home. And we can't take her on the train."

Boris knew Leonora was right, but he loved having Nessie by his side and rubbing her rough gray tummy. The Greycoats had horses back in Morovia, but they didn't have dogs–or even a grumpy cat like Tavish.

Boris filled his backpack with pebbles from his collection. It was time to return them to the beach.

"You're not really supposed to take things from the beach," Aileen had said, "even pebbles. And now that it's a nature reserve the rules are even stricter."

In the end, Boris was allowed to keep a few of his favorite pebbles, though Leonora said they needed to stay at Wolfemina Hall.

"We're not traveling home with them," she insisted.

So Boris had donated his collection, "Premium Scottish Pebbles, In Order of Smoothness," to the Wolfemina Hall Art Gallery.

Randall, Leonora and Aileen were having a meeting in the downstairs gallery.

"Do you think my pebble collection might be valuable one day?" Boris asked them.

"Mmm …" said Leonora. "If you painted portraits on all the pebbles, perhaps?"

Boris thought for a moment. "I don't have time for that," he said. "Also, I like pebbles better without pictures. Anyway, I'm going to the village to say goodbye to everyone."

"Only in the agony of parting," said Randall, in his quoting-aloud voice, "do we look into the depths of love."

"A little dramatic, my dear," said Leonora.

"I'm disappointed you're going, but I think it's best to leave when you're still enjoying yourself," said Aileen. "It will get cold soon!"

"Exactly," added Leonora. She was looking forward to tea on the lawn in sunny Morovia, away from gales and lashing rain.

Boris wandered along the beach until he found his favorite tide pool. He tipped his pebbles in.

Then he walked into town.

Boris popped in for a snack at the fish shop, and to say goodbye. The window advertised the "wolf special." For a tidy sum, you could get two dozen fish and a bucket each of scallops and prawns.

"Achyeelbeawathen," said the fishmonger, handing him a package of fresh prawns.

"Thank you," said Boris. "Yes, we will be away then."

He was getting better at "Scots Doric," as Randall said it was called.

The fishmonger grabbed a business card and handed it to him.

"Awawiyethen," he said. "Ahllmissyercustom."

"Thank you," said Boris, nibbling on a king prawn. "I will miss my custom too."

Next, Boris dropped in on Mrs. McKay at the café. He was in the mood for one of her chocolate eclairs with Highland cream.

"The council had a plaque made!" she told him cheerfully, as Boris licked the cream from his paws. "Look outside!"

She led him out the front and pointed at a black plaque with ornate gold writing.

"Famous cake shop, oft frequented by Scotland's first repatriated wolves," said the plaque.

"And I've added a sign to the window too," she said.

"It's wonderful," said Boris, giving her a hug.

Then he remembered his list.

"This is for the castle tea shop," he said, giving her a piece of paper with "Wolfemina Hall–suggested menu" written on it.

Mrs. McKay read it through and nodded. "A good selection. Something for everyone, and plenty of cake. I can certainly do this. Thank you, Boris!"

Next, Boris went to visit Murdo McMurtrie at his blacksmith's workshop.

Boris waited while Murdo pulled a Celtic sword from the fiery forge. The sword changed color from hot white to red to black as Murdo hammered it on his anvil.

"I'm supposed to be making railings," said Murdo, looking sheepish, "but I thought I'd slip in a sword or two, while the forge is going."

"I made something for you," he added, placing the sword on a rack to cool.

He dug in his pocket and handed Boris a key ring.

It had a sculpted metal fob in the exact shape of the wolf's head from the Stone of Crannoch.

Boris hugged it to his chest.

"It's wonderful," he said. "Thank you so much."

"It's great to see wolves back in Scotland," said Murdo, smiling. "Come back next summer!"

Letter to Portlessie

Back in Morovia, Boris sat in the garden under a pine tree. It was a warm autumn day and he was writing a letter in the dappled sunshine.

Dear Aileen,

We are back home at Greycoat Hall. It really does have twenty-three turrets, you know. I didn't think you believed me so I'm attaching a drawing so you can see how they all fit on.

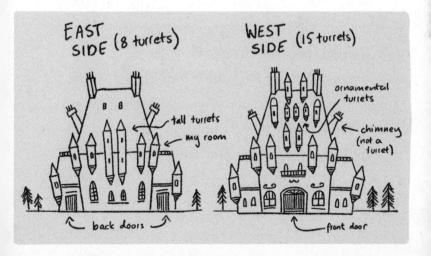

The journey home was very comfortable and I got to try cannoli on the train, and Dutch pancakes on the ferry.

I have told the cook at Greycoat Hall (who is also a wolf) how to make cakes with baking soda. The scones still taste of coconut, but at least they weigh less now. I miss Mrs. McKay's cakes.

I am also working on my new book, The Modern History of the Scottish Greycoats by Boris Greycoat. It will have cake recipes. Once the book is finished I will send a copy for the library at Wolfemina Hall.

Dad is learning Scottish blacksmithing, and has started his own battle reenactment society. He was learning to throw hammers, but Greycoat Hall has lots of windows so Mum said to take up a new hobby.

Mum is planning a vacation to somewhere warm for winter. She has made Celtic tea towels for the gift shop at Wolfemina Hall. They look really good.

Can you give the postcard to Jim? The picture on the front is the palace in Dukoprad, the capital of Morovia. It looks a bit different than Wolfemina Hall!

And the photo is for Irene, Jack and Ellie.

The building in the trees is my school. It's near our house so I can walk there. Some days, when I'm in a hurry, I ride to school on Vlad, my horse.

Please give Nessie a hug from me. Tell her I've put her portrait in my room. I miss her loads.

And maybe give Tavish a stroke from me, but only if he's in a good mood.

Much love,

Boris

PS: Can you make sure my pebble collection is properly displayed? I am worried that it should be arranged by size now, rather than smoothness. Sir Luther will know what to do, as I have explained my system to him.

Extract from
*A Guide to Scottish Baking
for the Morovian Wolf*

BORIS'S BANNOCKS

Ingredients:

- ★ 1 1/2 cups self-rising flour
- ★ A big pinch of baking soda
- ★ Pinch of salt
- ★ 1 tablespoon granulated sugar
- ★ 1 tablespoon fresh, creamy butter
- ★ 2 fresh eggs (beaten)
- ★ 1/2 cup milk

Note to the wolf chef: There is no need to add pig fat or coconut to this recipe.

Extra note: Be sure to remember the baking soda. It's a leavening agent and will make sure your bannocks are light and fluffy—not flat and rubbery.

Method:

Combine the flour, salt, sugar and baking soda in a large bowl. Make a hollow in the center of the flour mixture.

Now melt the butter in a large, heavy-bottomed frying pan or griddle. Then turn it off.

Pour the milk into the dry mixture, then tip in half the melted butter and half the beaten eggs.

Beat till smooth.

Add the rest of the eggs and mix till smooth (but more gently).

Heat the frying pan again and, once the butter is sizzling, drop large spoonfuls of your bannocks mixture onto it.

Once the tops of the bannocks start to bubble, flip them over with a spatula.

Wait a bit.

Take the bannocks out of the pan and arrange on a fancy plate. Serve with tea, jam and more butter.

Gobble them up, but remember to leave one or two for others.

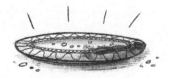

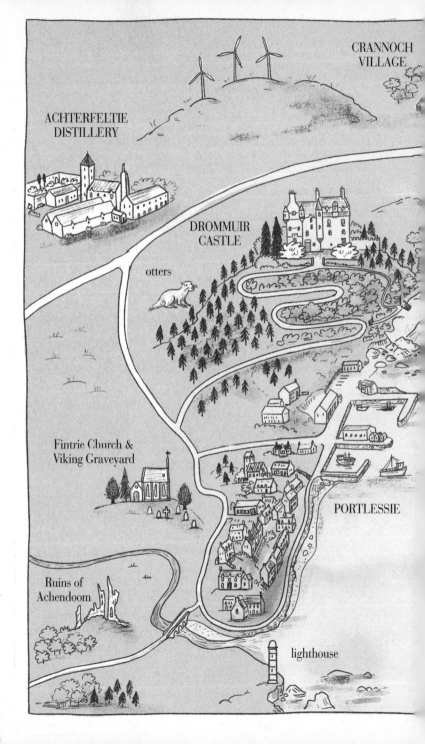

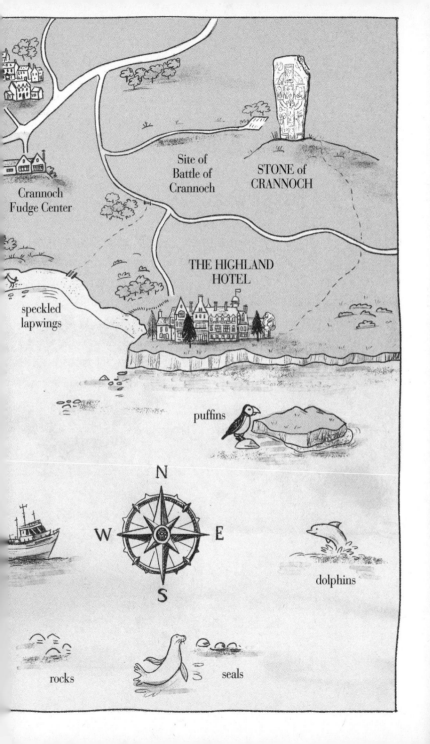

ACKNOWLEDGEMENTS

I'd like to thank my family, both Scottish and Australian, for inspiration, fact-checking and encouragement. A heartfelt thank you to Nancy Conescu for making Boris her pin-up wolf and for encouraging me to bring him to life. Thank you to Varuna, The Writers' House. A huge thank you to everyone who helped nurture the wolves into book form, especially Sarah Davis, Linsay Knight and the marvelous team at Walker, as well as my wonderful Thornbury writers' group and my agent Clare Forster at Curtis Brown.

Aroooooo**OOOOOO**ooooo!!!